THE BAFFLE BOOK

THE BAFFLE BOOK
STRIKES AGAIN

Fifteen Devilishly Difficult
Detective Puzzles

by

LASSITER WREN & RANDLE MCKAY

originators of the detective problem form

illustrated with diagrams and charts

DAVID R. GODINE · *Publisher*

Boston

This edition published in 2008 by
DAVID R. GODINE · Publisher
Post Office Box 450
Jaffrey, New Hampshire 03452
www.godine.com

Adapted from *The Baffle Book*, originally published in 1928
for the Crime Club, Inc., by Doubleday, Doran & Company, Inc.

LIBRARY OF CONGRESS
CATALOGING-IN-PUBLICATION DATA
Wren, Lassiter.
The baffle book strikes again : fifteen devilishly difficult detective
puzzles / by Lassiter Wren and Randle McKay.
p.   cm.
ISBN 978-1-56792-368-1
1. Detective and mystery stories.   2. Puzzles.
I. McKay, Randle. II. Title.
GV1511.D4W75   2008
793.73—dc22
2008024898

First Printing
PRINTED IN CANADA

WHAT IS YOUR SCORE FOR THE BAFFLE BOOK?

Score your credits here. A total of 75 is good. 100, excellent.
125, remarkable. 150 (maximum), amazing!

Carry forward ......

Answers to the questions printed at the end of each problem will be found in the Answer Section, printed upside-down in the back of the book. The highest possible score is 150 – that is, 10 credits each for the 15 mysteries or detective problems.

THE BAFFLE BOOK

FOR ALL WHO REVEL IN CRIME DETECTION

How OFTEN HAVE YOU been week-ending at the Duchess's place only to have the butler break in on the festive company with the tragic announcement that the master has been found slain in the billiard room, an Oriental dagger driven through his breast? And, fastened to the hilt by ribbon obviously from a wedding-cake box, a note – heliotrope-scented – on which is scrawled: "At last!" But the murderer has not signed it, and no one recognizes the handwriting. And there you are – everyone flabbergasted and in utter confusion. No one, not even the Homicide Squad, can make anything out of the clues, so the whole company, including yourself, is suspected of the crime.

A nice pickle to be in! And why? Simply because you never developed your latent powers of observation and deduction – those qualities of mind which make the solution of the most inscrutable mysteries a veritable pleasure. Confess it, you never heeded Conan Doyle; you thought it was all tosh. But it isn't, as this book will show.

A NEW AND CHALLENGING SPORT

The Baffle Book, with its mysteries and detective problems to be solved from given data and clues, will soon convert you to the enormous importance of observation and deduction. Solve a few of the hypothetical crime mysteries that follow and you will be equipped to work out any given crime at any given house-party at any given moment.

"What do you deduce?" will be the question on everyone's lips as soon as *The Baffle Book* reaches the public. Here are the evidences of the crime. These are the facts established by the police. What do you observe? Which are the telltale clues? What do you deduce? How will you answer the questions asked of you at the end of each mystery problem: "Who is guilty?" or "What motive?" etc. As you use your reasoning powers in the solution of each problem, so you will be rated according to the credits specified in the book. And if you are really baffled, then you can look up the true solution in the Answer Section in the back of the book. (To consult this, shut the book, turn it upside down and open the book again as usual. The answers are printed upside-down to deter you from looking too quickly for the solutions of the mysteries. It is more fun to work them out for yourself first.)

★　　★　　★

Introduction

YOU WILL BE BAFFLED

Most of the mysteries are not easy to solve at first glance. That is what makes them interesting. But each has a logical and absolute solution which can be deduced reasonably by any intelligent and well-informed person. You must consider all the circumstances of the crime or mystery as stated in the text or as given in the chart or diagram or illustration, if one accompanies the problem. Any, or all together, may yield the clue or clues essential for the unraveling of the mystery. Observe, deduce, reason it out. Don't guess or jump to conclusions; you will probably be wrong.

THE BAFFLE BOOK KEEPS FAITH

The mysteries propounded here are not trick puzzles or riddles with far-fetched answers to be guessed at. There are no trivial "catches" to mislead you. When the book says: "The police established the following as a fact" – the reader may accept that as a fact. The clues to the solution of the mystery are always there; it is for the reader to see them in their significance and to deduce from them in the light of the general situation.

In other words, *The Baffle Book* – unlike many detective stories – keeps faith with the reader by disclosing all the evidence that exists. It does not withhold vital facts for the purpose of baffling you. If the book asks:

"Was it the butler or the chauffeur who committed the crime?" you may assume that one or the other of them did, and you will not find the Answer Section lugging in the hitherto unsuspected ashman as the culprit.

THE IMPORTANCE OF THE SMALL CLUE

The seemingly trifling and insignificant clue may be the most revealing of all, and this is as it should be, for the annals of crime are filled with cases in which brilliant reasoning from faint clues has led to the solution of the mystery.

What could be more admirable than the celebrated feat of M. Goron, Prefect of Police in Paris forty years ago? A wealthy widow was reported missing from her home in the French capital, and foul play was suspected. She had disappeared one afternoon en route to a friend's house where she had promised to spend the night. She had never arrived at her destination. No trace of her could be found. Her nephews were suspected and shadowed. It looked very bad for her favorite nephew, for he stood to profit handsomely by her death.

Several months later a woman's body was found in a Paris park. Such was the condition of the corpse and clothing that not even the widow's servants could say definitely whether it was or was not the body of the widow. The servants ventured that it was, but the nephews said not. The mystery deepened.

Then M. Goron noticed that one of the nephews seemed less perturbed than might have been expected. The famous detective examined again the room of the missing widow and in a drawer found a soiled lace collar with a tiny brown spot on the back. The collar belonged to the widow, and the spot proved to be not blood but hair dye. It had been overlooked at first.

"So, then, your mistress dyed her hair, did she?" M. Goron said to a servant. "And how long had she been doing this?"

"She began about three months before she disappeared," was the reply.

M. Goron again examined the room and took inventory. He found no bottle of hair dye. All other possessions of the widow, except a nightgown, toothbrush, hairbrush and comb, were found in their proper places. The widow had gone, she said, to spend but one night at her friend's – and had never arrived.

"Why should she have taken the hair dye with her for merely an overnight visit?" M. Goron asked himself. She would not have done so, he thought. But she did take it, he reasoned back, and it was precious and essential to her. He deduced that she knew that she would be away longer than she had said.

Why would a rich widow secretly flee with hair dye? For a lover, and a young one, reasoned M. Goron. And he solved the case thereby, for the detective also reasoned that she must have a confidante in one of her nephews, and both were watched. The one upon whom suspicion of murder of his aunt had rested more heavily was caught mailing to her in London a fresh supply of the very same hair dye! It was essential to the widow's appearance in the eyes of the young Frenchman with whom she had fled four months before. The widow had wished to deceive everyone. The corpse was later identified as that of an Italian spy.

That was observation and reasoning triumphant!

Watch for similar subtleties in some of the mysteries to follow. *En garde!* Fifteen crimes have been committed awaiting your solution. What do you deduce?

HOW TO GIVE A BAFFLE PARTY

The Baffle Book grew out of a game. It lends itself well to use at any gathering or party. As devised by two mystery story writers to amuse studio gatherings in New York last winter, the game is sometimes called "Clues" or "Baffling Mysteries." So popular were these concocted mysteries with the players who tracked down the clues, that the best of the problems propounded have been put into book form by the originators. Now anyone can play merely with the aid of this book.

★　★　★

PLAYING SIDES

(Requiring two *Baffle Books*)

The host and hostess, or detective captains appointed by them, divide the group into two squads by choosing sides. Each team, armed with a *Baffle Book*, retires to an end of the room. At a given signal each begins work, simultaneously, on a certain mystery problem agreed upon. The team first solving a mystery announces it, without, of course, looking in the Answer Section. If right, the team gets all the credit specified in the book for answering the questions and a bonus of 10 besides (for speed). But if wrong, the team gets no credit and is penalized 5 for jumping to hasty conclusions. In short, *The Baffle Book* sets a premium on reasoning rather than guessing.

THE ONE-BOOK GAME

It is easy to amuse and baffle your friends by reading a problem to them aloud, slowly and distinctly. Give each player a pencil and paper in case he wants to take a note or two (although this is not necessary); but don't let anyone ask a question until you are through reading the data as given.

For purposes of a game a certain time is allotted for the solution of a problem – make it two or three or five minutes, as you prefer. Of course if everyone is baffled at the end of the first reading, you may reread the problem or parts of it – but only by unanimous consent of those playing. At the end of the allotted time you call a halt and read the solution from the Answer Section. Those who have been baffled and have written nothing down correctly score nothing. Those partly solving get credit for what they have done. Whoever gets the highest total score of the evening wins the title of Sherlock Holmes and is automatically licensed to carry a magnifying glass.

Naturally it always helps a Baffle Party if the host serves shag tobacco. Give a Baffle Party.

P.S.: It is considered the depth of infamy to spread the solutions to the mysteries around the office or neighborhood. Baffle someone with them first.

HINTS FOR SOLVING

Read the text of the mystery or detective problem carefully and consider the questions you are asked at the end of it.

If a diagram of the crime scene, or an illustration of any kind, accompanies the text of the mystery, examine that also for clues; it may give you a clue all by itself or it may tell you something which will further explain a clue in the text.

Sufficient clues from which the answers can be deduced are always to be found in the data given.

Introduction

Observe, deduce, reason out the solution – don't guess or jump to conclusions.

Don't admit you are baffled until you have spent at least five minutes on the shorter problems, or fifteen minutes apiece on the longer mysteries.

Even when you are baffled, try to answer some of the questions at the end of the problem before you look up the solution in the Answer Section.

To find the Answer Section, shut the book, turn it upside-down, and open again as usual; i.e., the Answer Section is printed upside-down.

For each question rightly answered, you gain certain credits. Mark these down as you go along, under "Credit Score."

NO. I

THE PROBLEM OF NAPOLEON'S SIGNATURES

What does handwriting tell you? Here is a pretty problem involving deductions from signatures of Napoleon Bonaparte penned at various crises in his amazing career. According to the late Hans Gross, famous authority on crime detection, it is possible to deduce from each autograph the state of Napoleon's mind and of his fortunes at the time of making.

REFERRING TO THE REVELATIONS of handwriting, Dr. Gross writes in his authoritative *Handbook of Criminal Investigation:*

The most difficult thing to do is to compare, not the writings of persons of different character but those of the same person in different moods. With much reason the various signatures of

Napoleon are usually cited in this connection. Few men have experienced so strongly as he the whole gamut of impressions. Few have seen so many events. . . . What changes in destiny! What changes of disposition! What changes *in writing!*

Study of the signatures is more instructive than a whole shelf full of books. It seems quite impossible to confound the dates of the various signatures and mistake those of the zenith of the fortunes of Bonaparte for that made at St. Helena.

On page 17 you will find facsimiles of eight authentic signatures of Napoleon I, made at various times. What do you deduce from them? What phases of his eventful career do they denote?

Dates of the signatures are withheld, but as a guide to solution of the problem, descriptive captions are given (one for each signature). It is for you to say if you can which caption belongs under each signature. This may be too difficult, however, for anyone but a handwriting expert, so the problem is confined to the following questions, which should be answered:

1. *Which was Napoleon's signature as General in Chief of the Egyptian Expedition in 1798 (before he became Emperor)?* (Credit 2.)

2. Which when he first became Emperor, in 1804*?* (Credit 3.)

3. Which at Tilsit in 1807 *(when all Europe but England lay at his mercy)?* (Credit 2.)

4. Which at Elba in 1814 *(his voluntary exile)?* (Credit 2.)

5. Which at St. Helena in 1815 *(the beginning of his enforced exile)?* (Credit 1.)

Credit Score:

The following captions indicate the varying states of mind and of the fortunes of Napoleon Bonaparte at the times of the making of the signatures. At various stages of his career, Napoleon signed himself differently: "N," "Bonaparte," "Napol.," "Napoleon," etc. Which signature belongs to what particular period? What do you deduce from the handwriting?

Before he became Emperor. Still a general. Written as Commander of the Egyptian Expedition in 1798.

Done very soon after becoming Emperor, in 1804. He had been First Consul or actual ruler of France for several years. Age 35.

A few days before his abdication as Emperor (just before voluntary exile on Elba). Done April 4, 1814.

Done two months after arriving at St. Helena on his forced and final exile. Date December, 1816.

At the Imperial Camp at Tilsit, 1807, when the Emperor had virtually all Europe, except England, at his mercy. Perhaps the climax of his military successes, but the beginning of the tremendous egotism of a world conqueror.

September, 1814. From the island of Elba where Napoleon went in voluntary exile. In a few months he retrieved his fortunes dramatically by returning. Then Waterloo.

Done at Berlin, October 29, 1806. At the very height of his career. In 1805 he had conquered Austria. In 1806, Prussia. He was still thinking clearly. Egotism had not yet dominated.

Done October 1, 1813. Bonaparte's enemies were slowly but surely wearing him down. Several of his armies commanded by his marshals had been defeated. Yet he was not to be beaten decisively until 1815.

NO. 2

THE GREAT IMPERIAL BANK ROBBERY

IF LATE NOVEMBER OF 1926 had not been unsea-
sonably warm, or if Lieutenant Elkins of the Ottawa
police had not been so observant, it is almost certain
that the resourceful robbers of the Imperial Bank of
the Canadian capital would have escaped punish-
ment. As it was, though the bandits themselves were
captured, their confederates escaped and the money
was never recovered.

The robbery had been well planned. As Lieutenant
Elkins afterward established, the four bandits entered
the bank soon after the opening hour. McCrory, the
leader, was effectively disguised as a crippled war
veteran, limping with a hesitancy which was soon
abandoned in the swift action that followed. His com-
panions were conventionally garbed in blue suits, each
wearing a false beard or moustache; and two wore
spectacles.

The alluring objective was the acquisition of three large factory payrolls which the robbers knew were being prepared at that hour for representatives of the factories. These, totaling $54,000, were swept into bags within a few seconds of the beginning of the well-timed and cold-blooded assault. The men dashed out, leaped into a black racing car, and were around the corner before anyone dared to spread the alarm. Police followed in commandeered cars, but they lost the trail within a few minutes in the morning traffic and were baffled to know which way to proceed.

Ten minutes later police headquarters received word from a suburban section that an automobile containing four men was speeding on one of the highways to the north of the city. Lieutenant Elkins was rushed to the spot and picked up there a brief description of the car. The informant was able to point out the exact tracks made by the car. Lieutenant Elkins followed them, having left instructions to telephone ahead to all possible destinations on the road taken by the speeding car and have police of the various communities head it off.

There was little difficulty in following the track of the car. Its distinctive tire impressions led seven miles due north on the main highway, then a mile to the west on the broad, dusty Derham road flanked by level meadows. At this point the car's tracks mingled with other tire tracks, which baffled the pursuers for a distance of about a third of a mile.

However, certain that the fleeing car could have gone on in only one way, Elkins directed his driver to forge ahead, and at the end of the one-third mile stretch the car's distinctive tracks again appeared alone in the road.

A few minutes later he reached the town of Derham and there learned that a touring car containing four men had driven through in leisurely fashion twenty minutes before. Their descriptions, however, differed so radically from those broadcast by the Ottawa police that the local constable had not interfered with them. None had a beard or moustache or glasses, and all four were chatting gaily. They had been observed by several persons, and a fair description had been gleaned: two wore light gray tweed suits and overcoats; the other two, brown clothes. They were young, and the constable had taken them for college students on an outing.

Lieutenant Elkins wisely telephoned ahead to Wheatonville and had them arrested on suspicion. They indignantly denied all knowledge of the crime and invited search of their persons and of the automobile. Nothing whatever incriminating was found. Lieutenant Elkins managed to have them held, however, until he had time to investigate further the con-

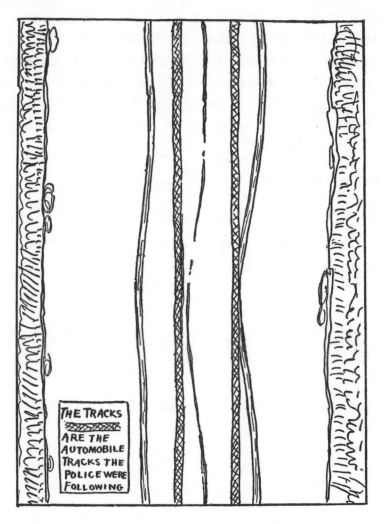

Segment of the broad, dusty Derham road showing mysterious tracks discovered by Lieutenant Elkins in pursuing the robbers of the Imperial Bank.
Grass at extreme left and right.

fusion of tire tracks which had baffled him back on the Derham road. After some thought and study the mystery was explained. A diagrammatic sketch of a section of the Derham road is shown on page 21.

What do you deduce? What had happened? The questions to be answered are:

1. *What had happened on the Derham road where the confusion of tire tracks baffled Elkins?* (Credit 7.)

2. *What step should a good detective have taken immediately in an effort to recover the money?* (Credit 3.)

Credit Score:

NO. 3

THE PROBLEM
AT THE ABANDONED
BUNGALOW

TOWARD THE END OF A DAY in the summer of
1927, the police of Seattle received a tip from underworld sources that a gang of alleged bank robbers
might be found at a certain abandoned bungalow on
the outskirts of the city. In spite of elaborate precau-
tions of the police, who hoped to surprise the gang,
the bungalow when surrounded was found deserted.
The occupants had apparently been tipped off in their
turn by someone who knew what was to happen.

It was a one-room bungalow, long since abandoned
by its owners. Almost all the furniture had been removed. The detectives were confronted by the problem
of deducing, from the evidence in the room, the size
of the gang and some characteristics of its members.

The room was furnished merely with four kitchen

chairs, a wooden packing box, a rickety table, and some old crockery. The only clues available were as follows:

Besides many matches of the ordinary paper type on the floor about the table, there were twenty-odd burned, large-sized wooden matches scattered on the floor behind one of the chairs.

Stubs of five Turkish cigarettes and four cigarettes made from Virginia tobacco.

One cigar butt, Corona-Perfecto.

The four chairs and the wooden packing box placed around the table as shown in the accompanying sketch.

A bottle of iodine, nine tenths full, with several drops of iodine on the seat of the chair on which it stood.

The cigarette- and cigar-stubs were scattered, some on the floor, some by the cups that stood on the table.

Closer examination of the cups showed that they had contained a good brand of whiskey. Clearly defined on the wooden packing box were a dozen or more small dents, equally divided into two groups about six inches apart – both groups some eight inches from the floor. The dents were each about a quarter of an inch

Sketch from police photographs of the scene at the abandoned bungalow. (Courtesy of Capt. Farnsworth.)

long and less than a sixteenth of an inch deep in the soft wood. The cigar butt was found by the cup in front of the wooden box.

Neither footprints nor fingerprints were in evidence. Nevertheless, the detectives were able to infer important characteristics of some of the occupants of the bungalow. Ultimately it resulted in the identification and capture of the gang.

Had you been there as a detective, what would you have deduced? The questions to be answered are:

1. *How many were in the gang?* (Credit 2.)

2. *What was a distinguishing characteristic of each member which might serve to identify the gang if seen by the police?* (Credit 8.)

Credit Score:

NO. 4

THE WARFIELD-COBHAM JEWEL ROBBERY

Just one question concerned the police in the Warfield-Cobham case: was the butler an accomplice? How would you have answered it?

THE EARLY EDITIONS of the Chicago afternoon newspapers of Thursday, July 23rd, carried the first news of the robbery of Mrs. Henry Warfield-Cobham's summer home. It was the sensation of the month. The wealthy widow, who had lived in virtual retirement since the death of her distinguished husband four years before, had been found that morning humanely but efficiently gagged and bound in her own bed, having been an eyewitness during the night to a $60,000 jewel robbery in her own bedroom on the second floor. A wall safe at the back of her bureau had been forced with chisel and crowbar before her eyes and emptied of its contents by a tall, broad-shouldered and courteous individual who was immediately spotted by the police from her description, as "Gentleman Claude," alias François Marchesne, the notorious Quebec cracksman commonly alleged to have done equal time in prison and college. At any rate, the police said, the job had been done with the consummate courtesy characteristic of "Gentleman Claude" – and the jewels were gone.

The police were inclined to believe that the robber must have had information, if not actual assistance, from someone on the inside of the house. But on this point Mrs. Warfield-Cobham was firm: she refused to believe that any of her staff of old servants could have been implicated in the robbery. Present during the detectives' questioning of them all, the lady of the house openly expressed confidence in the integrity of each. Each of the servants denied any knowledge of the affair, and, apparently, with the deepest sincerity. The police were nettled.

Early in the afternoon following the robbery, however, a paint salesman of Rivington – a town near the Warfield-Cobham summer home – came to the police with the following story:

I was walking along the Rivington road last night about twelve o'clock, wheeling my motor-cycle. It had broken down. I saw a sedan car in the woods opposite a big estate. It was driven up into the bushes so far, it looked as if someone wanted to hide it. I went up and looked at it, and it was a Buick sedan. Nobody was in it. I went on my way a hundred feet or so, and I thought I saw a man drop over the big wall of the estate.

I didn't know whose estate it was. I waited awhile and laid down my machine and climbed up a tree. In the moonlight I could see the figure of a man moving stealthily from bush to bush, going toward the house. It was a big house. The man was very tall. I could see him but he didn't see me. He was carrying something in his left hand about the size of a big club.

All of a sudden, while he was waiting behind a bush, a light flashed, up near the top of the house. It flashed twice more – from up near the eaves. Then the big fellow stepped right out and walked boldly across the lawn and went around the side of the house. So I thought it must be all right – perhaps some lover or an elopement or something. I never thought it could be a robbery, because the light signals were so plain. But now I have read the papers and seen the picture of the house in the papers, and it was the Warfield-Cobham house all right. I wish I hadn't gone home so soon. I didn't hear any noise after that. I went on.

As a result of this report the police shadowed the Warfield-Cobham servants for more than two weeks, but to no avail. Butler, gardener, chauffeur, cook, housekeeper, maids – by all their actions they were conventional and law-abiding individuals.

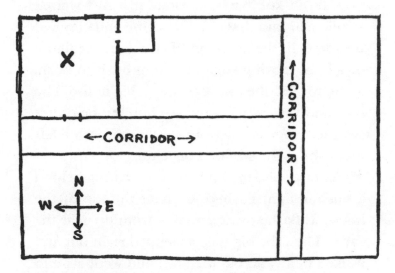

Floor plan of the second floor of Warfield-Cobham house.
X marks the bedroom of Mrs. Warfield-Cobham.

But finally there came to the police through that invisible telegraph system of the underworld – the stool pigeon – a vague tip that the butler, John Ardmore, had known "Gentleman Claude" of old. And Detective Sergeant Hodge, newly assigned to the case, managed to strike up a flirtation with one of the maids without revealing that he was a detective. In the course of time he learned that Ardmore, on the Tuesday before the robbery, had sent a letter from the summer home into Chicago (thirty-one miles) by the chauffeur!

The chauffeur, cornered by Hodge and two other detectives in Chicago that evening, readily admitted taking the letter. But he said that it could have had nothing to do with the robbery since it contained an advertisement to be inserted in the Chicago Daily *Sun*. He said he had delivered it at one of the *Sun* branch offices as requested by the butler. It had contained a money order to pay for the advertisement, he said, and the envelope was addressed to the "Want Ad." Dept.

The chauffeur added:

> John told me the letter was important and must be delivered at once. He said a friend had asked him to mail it a few days ago and that he had forgotten to do it. The writing on the envelope wasn't like John's. I think you're all crazy. Check it up at the newspaper office and you'll find that it was nothing but an ad.

Taking the chauffeur with him, Detective Sergeant Hodge went to the branch office of the *Sun*. The clerks there could give no clue as to *which* of the thousands of want ads received on that particular day had come

31

from the letter said to have been delivered by the chauffeur. But Hodge persevered. He searched all the columns of the *Sun*, a morning paper, of the day of the robbery. He found six advertisements which he decided were unusual enough to warrant a thorough examination for hidden meaning.

From the ads. herewith reproduced, Sergeant Hodge reached a very definite conclusion. What would you have deduced?

The questions to be answered are:

1. *Was the butler an accomplice in the robbery?* (Credit 1.)

2. *How could the detective be certain of the conclusion he reached?* (Credit 9.)

Credit Score:

SITUATIONS WANTED, MALE

MANAGER'S ASSISTANT, varied experience, just back from tour made for government bureau, desires return commercial life preferably Northwest or Middle West; competent act second in command event manager's absence; business immaterial provided only that it offers a living salary and lucrative opportunity advancement within couple years. Available Wednesday. Wide general experience. Address Box 12 Central Post Office, Minneapolis.

HELP WANTED, MALE

REAL ESTATE SALESMEN can earn big money selling shrubbery, evergreens, trees, roses, &c., for planting next Fall or Spring: free plans for landscape jobs, large and small; every home a prospect; no collecting; buyers pay after delivery; complete line of highest grade goods; wonderful selling material and full coöperation; orders run big; one sale leads to more; excellent opportunity to connect permanently for full or part time on liberal commission basis with nationally known highly rated concern; this is a fine proposition. Y 2182. *The Sun.*

MANAGER FOR BROADCASTING STATION. A nationally known firm is desirous of securing the services of a manager for a broadcasting station; must be a high type executive capable of sales results; the man accepted will have to pass a rigid test as to character and responsibility; knowledge of the broadcasting field is desirable but not necessary; successful sales ability is required; send all information possible in first letter stating age, whether married or single, amount of insurance carried and membership in fraternal organizations. Z 2483. *The Sun.*

THERE IS available a most desirable connection for a salesman who is of the bigger type, who can intelligently present a unique service of extraordinary merit; the opportunity is with a highly successful organization, leaders in their field, with a high reputation for a quality product and a capable executive staff; previous advertising experience not necessary, but ability above the average is decidedly important; the type of man we seek may be employed at present and may feel skeptical about answering a blind advertisement, but you will find it worth while to satisfy us that you are big enough and interview will be arranged; the position requires traveling in assigned territory; man who has earned $8,500 upward; commission and drawing account basis. Address A. M., 1210 New Street, La Grange, Ill.

HELP WANTED, FEMALE

YOUNG LADY, brunette, age not over twenty-five, weight not over 120 pounds, height about five feet, must be of pleasing personality, able and willing to appear in public places attired in French aviation costume for advertising purposes, account of exclusive hotel must furnish references. Z 2270. *The Sun.*

BUSINESS CONNECTIONS

GERMAN MERCHANT, Partner of old established Hamburg firm, with sales organization and first-class connections all over Germany and Morocco (North Africa); at present on short visit in this city; is desirous of taking up negotiations, representation of high-class American concerns wanting an outlet in above countries also open for any other propositions to represent American interests in Germany. B 31. *The Sun.*

The unusual want ads. selected by Detective Hodge

NO. 5

THE LA JOYA RIVER HOMICIDE

Where Portos da Vega, the La Joya cowboy, met his death, the State police finally learned by very sensible methods of deduction. But they never caught the murderer because they did not determine quickly enough from which ranch his body had been thrown into the river. The slayer escaped and has never been heard of to this day. How would you have solved the problem which then confronted the State police?

EARLY ON THE MORNING of October 4th mill hands at the La Joya mill saw a dark object washed over the low dam of the river and become lodged between two rocks only fifty yards from the east bank of the river. They investigated and found that it was the body of a man, and brought it ashore at 6:20 A.M. The actual time of the sighting of the body as it washed over the dam was established as 6:13.

It proved to be the strangled body of Portos da Vega, a daring horseman and crack shot who had previously worked at various times for many of the ranchers whose ranches abutted on the river. Since all the ranches were on the east side of the river, and since the body came down so close to the east bank, it seemed clear that the victim had been thrown into the water from one of the ranches. It was also clear that the man had been strangled by a piece of rope before having entered the water. The coroner found no water in the lungs; the body had been floating.

The coroner pronounced that the body had been in the water "not less than 40 minutes and not more than four hours," and that death had occurred before immersion. A search of the dead man's pockets yielded two illuminating clues: his watch and a scrap of paper. The watch was a cheap one of standard make. Its water-soaked hands pointed to 5:25, and it proved to be nearly wound up – lacking only three turns from being fully wound. From tests made on the spot with other watches of the same brand and type it was determined that Da Vega's watch must have stopped within two to four minutes after immersion.

In the dead man's breeches pocket was found a small ball of paper, a fragment of a note handwritten in capital letters with a blue crayon pencil. Though soaked and smeared it was recognizable. The fragment said:

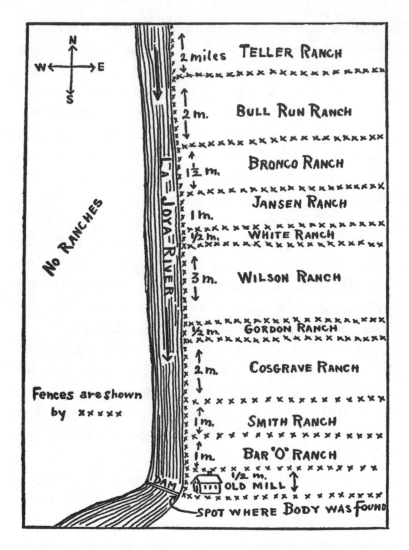

Rough map of La Joya River region furnished to the State police by the county engineer.

RANCH NORTHWEST CORNER BY RIVER FENCE, AT 5:15 TOMORROW MORNING IF YOU WANT THE STRAIGHT DOPE ON LA MOLLURA.

                                                    A FRIEND

Now, it was well known that by "La Mollura" the unknown writer of the message had meant Molly Sanders, a girl of easy virtue who was a sort of "college widow" with the ranchers of the La Joya region. Intrigues and quarrels over her were frequent, but this looked like murder, for Da Vega was a chivalrous though distant admirer of Molly and had been known to resent the general slurs cast upon her by various men.

Accordingly the State police obtained from the county engineer a rough map of the region, and the speed of the river current on the east side. This was found to be six miles an hour. The engineer said that the river was without snags or impediments on the east bank for a distance of eleven miles.

Had you been a detective, on which ranch would you have said that Portos da Vega probably met his death?

The question to be answered is:

To which ranch would you have directed the search for further clues? (Credit 10.)

Credit Score:

NO. 6

THE DUVENANT
KIDNAPPING CASE

WHEN RICHARD DUVENANT brought suit for divorce
against his wife, the former Dorothy Willington, in
1924, naming as co-respondent an Italian count, the
New York tabloids added materially to their circula-
tions. It will be remembered that Duvenant won his
suit and received from the court the custody of the
two children, Fletcher, eight, and Jonathan, four, in
spite of their mother's frantic battle to keep at least
one of them. This was in May, 1924. The aftermath of
the suit, the kidnapping of Jonathan, the younger child,
came two months later. Since news of the kidnapping
has never yet been published, and since the affair
involved a remarkable piece of deduction by one of
the Duvenant private detectives, the details are here
recounted for the first time.

After the divorce Duvenant retained his magnificent estate in the Orange Mountains of New Jersey,

commuting daily to his Wall Street office. Early in the afternoon of July 14th he received a telephone call from Thelma Lanssen, Swedish governess to his children, who was in charge of them at the New Jersey estate. She was almost incoherent in her terrified announcement that the two boys had both disappeared while playing in the grounds of the estate twenty minutes before. Chauffeur, gardener, and all other servants were engaged in a frantic search of the countryside. Duvenant ordered that the police be notified and said that he was starting home at once. He then telephoned to the Norcross Detective Agency of Newark, New Jersey, five miles from his estate, and requested that operatives be rushed to his home by automobile. Duvenant reached home a little after three and found John Norcross himself already in charge of the investigations on the grounds. Fletcher, the older boy, had been found by the gardener, but Jonathan, his mother's favorite, was missing. Fletcher told the following story.

He and Jonathan had been playing Indians, and he was hiding in ambush in the tool house while Jonathan was to ride up on his velocipede and be attacked and scalped. He had waited a long time in the back of the toolhouse, from which point he could see nothing outside, and when Jackie did not arrive to be scalped he had tired of the game and gone to open

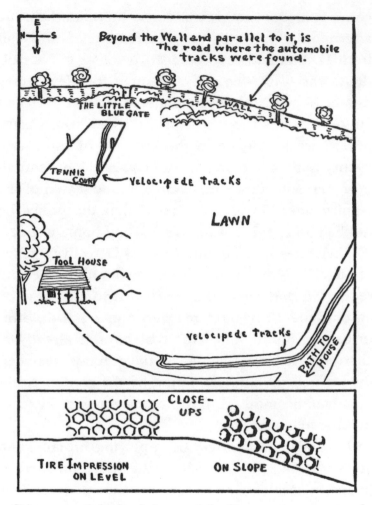

Diagram of the back lawn of the Duvenant estate and close-ups of tire impressions on the road.

the door. He found it locked. The toolhouse locked with a padlock on the outside. Fletcher thought that the little chap had locked him in for a joke, and, therefore, made no noise for some minutes, pretending that he did not care in order that Jackie would be disappointed. But in a few minutes he had grown impatient and had wailed and kicked on the door. After what must have been twenty minutes, his screams were heard by the gardener, who was passing, and he was released.

Duvenant and Detective Norcross found the wheel tracks of Jonathan's velocipede across the tennis court, as shown on the diagram on page 40. The trail led to the gate at the back of the extensive lawn of the estate, the same "little blue gate," in fact, which had figured so prominently in the tabloid accounts of the Duvenant divorce trial. Deep in the thick bushes to the left of the gate Jonathan's velocipede was found. The footprints of a woman and the footprints of Jonathan leading out of the little gate were found. The gate was locked. On the soft dirt road on which the Duvenant estate backed were found the clearly defined tire impressions of a large automobile. There could be no doubt that Jonathan had been persuaded into the automobile and that it had disappeared, bearing him away. Neither could there be any doubt in Duvenant's mind that his divorced wife had done the deed. Whoever had fetched the child had had a key to the Yale lock which prevented the casual by-passer from opening the gate. White with anger, Duvenant swore to pursue the kidnapper and retrieve the child. His magnificent Fiat car was prepared for the pursuit. But which way had the kidnapper gone, north or south? The road along which the car had traveled ran up a fairly steep slope for 200 yards to the little blue gate, and then ran level. Detective Norcross and Duvenant inspected the tire tracks closely. Duvenant said that there was nothing to tell whether the kidnapping car had approached from the south and gone north, or vice versa, for the track passed without turning.

This point happened to be of the greatest importance, for the road led north direct to New York and south to Philadelphia. It was a Friday and Duvenant feared that his former wife might be planning to leave the country that night by one of the Friday midnight steamers from New York. A southward journey, on the other hand, probably meant a journey to her father's estate in southern New Jersey, where concealment of the child would be easy. In either case, to head off or overtake the kidnappers was highly desirable in order to avoid recourse to the law. Which way had the car gone – north or south?

Detective Norcross rose to the occasion and deduced it from an examination of the auto tracks.

Had you been confronted with such a problem, what would you have said?

The questions to be answered are:

1. *In which direction did the kidnapper's car depart from the little blue gate — to the north or to the south?* (Credit 3.)

2. *What proved the direction taken by the car?* (Credit 7.)

Credit Score:

NO. 7

THE LIGHTHOUSE TRAGEDY AT DEAD MAN'S HARBOR

AT DEAD MAN'S HARBOR on the Bay of Fundy there is an isolated village with a population of not more than two hundred persons. At high tide the village is based upon a rocky peninsula which rises sheer, twenty feet above the water.

But when the great forty-foot tide rushes out, it leaves the village on a promontory sixty feet in the air; while the island of the lighthouse, almost circular in shape, rises like a great, squat cylinder, nearly forty-three feet above the flat sands.

At ebb tide, for the space of forty minutes, it is possible to cross dry-shod from village to island. Reeled wire ladders, let down the rock, permit descent from the village to the sands below. One can cross to the island and ascend by similar means the almost perpendicular sides of the rock where a level green lawn surrounds the old lighthouse.

The island in Dead Man's Harbor is lonely enough when surrounded by the whipping waters of the bay, but when the cruel rocks rise steeply from the wet sands below it is grim indeed.

On the night of the strange disappearance of Captain Ebenezer Williams, veteran keeper of the lighthouse, high tide came at 11:51, long after Daniel Cobb, the captain's helper, had gone to his home in the village. A heavy fog had settled on the harbor just before eleven o'clock, and the weird moan of the foghorn broke the night with a dismal regularity.

The following morning Daniel Cobb, coming soon after low tide, as was his custom, to relieve the captain, climbed down the ladder on the face of the cliff to cross the sands to the lighthouse. He noticed a broad trail in the hard-packed, damp sand – as though a board some fifteen inches wide had been dragged over the surface. The impression, Cobb said, was not deep. The board, if it was a board, seemed to have been dragged rather lightly over the sand. The trail ran from the foot of the ladder at the cliff straight to the cliffs of the lighthouse island.

Cobb entered the lighthouse at 6:01 A.M. He called to the captain and started upstairs. There was no answer. He went to look for him. The captain was not in the lighthouse, nor anywhere on the tiny island. Mystified, Cobb ran to the little boathouse expecting to find the captain's boat gone, only to discover the boat stored away with the oars in their usual place, all dry. The island is less than ninety yards in diameter and is covered with a close-cropped lawn. There was no other place for anyone to hide!

Cobb shouted everywhere and searched diligently in every conceivable place, but there was no trace of Captain Williams. Cobb, it may be stated, was promptly and justifiably exonerated of all suspicion by the examining police; he was of excellent character and deeply attached to the captain.

Cobb then rushed to the edge of the island and peered down the steep sides, but nowhere on the smooth rocks or in the telltale expanse of wet sand which surrounded the island completely were any traces whatever except for the fifteen-inch-wide trail which he had observed before reaching the island.

Cobb summoned aid from the village, and searching parties were sent out, since it was unprecedented for the captain to have left the lighthouse untended. The local constable, with Cobb and several villagers, made a thorough examination of the island and the lighthouse. They could find no trace from which a struggle or foul play could be deduced. They remarked that the foghorn was still blowing, although the fog had lifted that morning a few minutes before low tide. The engine of the foghorn, which had to be refueled every two hours, still had enough gasoline on hand at 6:05 A.M. (when Cobb examined it) to last for nearly another hour.

By 6:20 A.M. the tide was beginning to wash in in earnest. The entire party, therefore, made a minute examination of the single trail to ascertain whether there were any footprints near it. None could be found. Hours went by. It was a mystery – inexplicable, baffling, and to some of the superstitious sailors and fishermen of the village, terrifying. The captain, although he was not a popular man and led an existence much aloof from the villagers, was not known to have any enemies; while no one knew much of his former life, he had been a respected member of the community for eleven years. Where had he gone? The villagers even went to such lengths as to inspect carefully the soil and sod of the island to see if a body might have been cleverly concealed; but there were no traces. Nor could anyone be found to defend the theory that the captain, strictly devoted to his governmental duty, could have suddenly decided to abandon his post without explanation. Assuming that there had been foul play, it was highly improbable that the murderer, having dragged his victim's corpse across to the cliff base, would have carried it up the ladder and through the

The promontory and the lighthouse island at low tide.

The promontory and the lighthouse island at high tide.

single street of the village, as he would have to do to reach the wooded portions of the promontory. Search everywhere in the neighborhood proved fruitless.

Now it happened that a former official of the French Sûreté Générale, the Scotland Yard of France, was visiting at one of the summer homes in the vicinity – M. Eugène Jacques, who is credited with the solution of the celebrated D'Ormes case of Marseilles. Having heard of the strange disappearance of the captain, he came to the island. Delighted at the interest of so celebrated a detective, the constable requested him to examine the scene and the witnesses, and to pronounce an opinion on the mystery. After a half-hour examination had yielded the facts which have been stated, and after familiarizing himself with the locale of the mystery, the French detective startled everyone by pronouncing it a case of cold-blooded murder. "Murder," M. Jacques stated with the greatest confidence, "by someone who had planned the crime most carefully." The foreigner even predicted the circumstances under which the body of the captain would be found, and with remarkable astuteness reconstructed many of the events of the tragedy.

Two weeks later his predictions concerning the finding of the body proved correct. The mysterious assailant of the captain was subsequently captured, although this was more the result of extreme good luck on the part of the Scranton, Pennsylvania, police than anything else.

The questions to be answered are:

1. *How did M. Jacques know that it was murder?* (Credit 1.)

2. *How did the murderer probably reach the island?* (Credit 2.)

3. *How did he dispose of the body of Captain Williams?* (Credit 2.)

4. *How did he escape from the island?* (Credit 3.)

5. *Under what circumstances would the captain's body probably be found?* (Credit 2.)

Credit Score:

NO. 8

WHO MURDERED ALGERNON ASHE?

In crime detection the seemingly insignificant clue often proves to be of the greatest importance. Such a clue ultimately led to the capture of the murderer of Algernon Ashe. Had you been there as detective, what would you have deduced?

THE BODY OF ALGERNON ASHE was found soon after dawn one morning in late July, 1926, in shrubbery of the beautiful gardens not far from the Monte Carlo Casino. Ashe was an Englishman, a professional gambler and something of a Lothario. He had been stopping at a prominent Monte Carlo hotel for several weeks.

The *gendarmes* who discovered the body noted the following facts. Ashe had been killed by a pistol bullet through the heart, shot from behind. Death had been almost instantaneous. There were no powder marks on the clothes. The pockets of the coat and trousers obviously had been searched, but a large sum of cash and a valuable gold watch had been left. No weapon was found. The man had been dead, they established, at least six hours.

Many footprints, all of them fitting the victim's shoes, indicated that Ashe had walked up and down before a large bush, as if waiting for someone. Two cigarette stubs found in the grass nearby bore out the theory of his having waited, for they were of the same distinctive English brand as those in his cigarette case. Evidently he had waited some time.

A careful search of the entire region of the crime scene revealed the following clues: one burned match; one flat paper match-container (*empty*) of a common French type; one fragment of soft, thin cardboard, partially burned. Printing in English on both sides of the fragment was legible. Both sides of the fragment are reproduced on the next page.

Detectives assigned to the case shrewdly deduced that these had been left by the murderer. Ashe probably had not used the match to light a cigarette because a well-worn patent lighter was found in his vest pocket. The previous night had been an unusually dark one, and a light would have been almost essential to a quick search of packets. The detectives reasoned that the murderer had struck his last match to make the search, had not finished when the match had burned well down, and had then improvised another match from a bit of cardboard – lighting it from the match. The match was burned down to an eighth of an inch. But a whole inch of the cardboard fragment remained unburned.

Where had the cardboard come from? Had the murderer, in his haste to find something to ignite before his last match went out, taken it from his own pocket? Probably so, the detectives reasoned, for a man in the murderer's predicament might be expected to seize the first available bit of paper, provided it was not a valuable paper. The fact that he had discarded it when through indicated that it was not valuable to him; further, that he never considered it a dangerous clue.

Puzzling over the meaning of the fragment, of which they could make nothing, the detectives went to the hotel where Ashe had stayed. They found there a letter for the victim. It had come in the early mail. The postmark proved it had been mailed sometime before eleven of the night before in Monte Carlo. Hastily scrawled in a woman's hand, it ran:

A. DEAREST!

At the last minute I cannot come! I am desolated but it cannot be helped. For some reason he left the tables early and has just told me to pack at once. We leave in an hour. It is the bank stock matter. But I will be back in four days at the most and then India, or Brazil, or anywhere, A. darling, with you. Not more than five days at the most. Will try to get this to you by messenger if it doesn't seem dangerous. If so, will mail. I love you.

Yours forever,
M.

The detectives set about their difficult task of tracing a woman whose name or nickname might begin with M. – whose male escort had hurried her off to somewhere the night before – who wrote English. But the traffic out of Monte Carlo each day was enormous. Which of the hundreds of departing visitors was she and where had she gone? Examination of many hotel records and the departure records kept by the police yielded no conclusive information on the identity of the woman who had penned the note. Out of hundreds the detectives settled on three parties of travelers as suspects:

MAUDE RHONDA and HOLMHURST RHONDA, daughter and father, of London; departed for Spain.

MARY FREEMAN and FREDERIC FREEMAN, wife and husband, of Buffalo, N. Y.; departed for Paris.

MIRIAM DE RUYTER, LOUISA DE RUYTER, ANDREAS DE RUYTER and SIMON DE RUYTER, two sisters and their brother and father, of Rotterdam, Holland; departed for Rome.

All had departed the previous night. Inquiry at the various hotels where they had stopped yielded no conclusive clues. The De Ruyter family, like most educated Hollanders, spoke English perfectly. It was ascertained that the father was old and feeble and had been confined to his room that evening until departing. The brother, however, described as a dapper stripling by hotel servants, had been at the casino and had returned early, telling a servant that he had been unlucky again. After visiting the family's apartment he had again gone out. Nothing else could be learned.

Information about the Rhondas and the Freemans was even more difficult to obtain. Attendants at their hotel described Maude Rhonda as beautiful, statuesque, quiet; her father as "stern and even grim, a short, slight man who limped in the left leg, with gray moustache and hair." The Freemans were well dressed young Americans, apparently with money. Neither had attracted special attention at their hotel. The wife was described as pretty, bright, and petite; the husband as quiet, self-contained – "a tall, stout man, smooth-shaven." Both Freemans were in their early twenties. Nothing could be learned of the movements of the Rhondas or Freemans prior to their departure.

The detectives were in a quandary. Their investigation had yielded nothing to go on. Should they follow all three suspected parties to their destinations? Two of them would prove wild-goose chases, and much time would be lost. They must narrow down the search. This they did by seeking the advice of a famous detective who had traveled widely both in England and America. From the data you now have had he deduced which of the three parties contained the murderer. The detectives followed his advice and ultimately captured their man. The prisoner broke down when his actions at the scene of the crime were reconstructed before him by the detectives, and he later confessed the murder of Ashe.

Which party would you have followed? The questions to be answered are:

1. *Who murdered Algernon Ashe?* (Credit 1.)

2. *How did the detective deduce it?* (Credit 9.)

Credit Score:

NO. 9

ÉDOUARD TRIMPI'S PERPLEXING DISPATCH

What did Trimpi's dispatch mean and why was he arrested?
Baffling at first glance, it is really a simple problem.

AT 9:30 ON THE MORNING of April 13th the cable editor of the New York *Evening Chronicle* was surprised to receive a cablegram from Barcelona, Spain, evidently sent by Édouard Trimpi, the *Chronicle's* celebrated Paris correspondent, then on sick leave in Spain.

It is reproduced here:

> BARCELONA APR 12
> PRESS COLLECT
>
> NEWCHRON
> [New York Chronicle, New York.]
> ÉDOUARD EGO, REGARDED AS THOROUGH-
> LY COMPETENT FINANCIAL OBSERVER, TODAY

GRANTED ME FOLLOWING INTERVIEW: "COM-
PLETE MARKET OVERTURN IS IMMINENT ON
ACCOUNT OF ACCUMULATED LACK OF POPU-
LAR BUYING OF CHAIR SHARES PLUS SHARP
RISE STEEL. LATTER BOUNDED TODAY COR-
NERING SEVERAL HUNDRED OPERATORS WHO
WERE SEEKING TO CHECK CHAIR SHARE
DECLINE. SUCH SEEMS IMPOSSIBLE BECUASE
CURB BUYING TODAY WITH STEEL AS FAVORITE
WAS TUMULTUOUS." ANOTHER INTERVIEW
PROMISED TOMORROW.

TRIMPI.

Had Trimpi sent the dispatch? Nothing was expected
from him. His regular post was in Paris and his presence in Spain on sick leave a mere matter of chance.
He was not a financial expert. The *Chronicle*'s regular
Spanish correspondent was in Madrid, in another
part of Spain. Nothing had come from him for a week;
but the news out of Spain was not frequent.

The editors checked back on the cable company
and found that the dispatch had been correctly transmitted. Since they had no prearranged code with their
correspondents several of the editors reached the conclusion that someone was playing a joke.

Others dissented. While debating the matter, the
Chronicle received a wire from the State Department

in Washington, informing it of the bare fact that Trimpi had been taken into custody by the Spanish authorities and was being held incommunicado. This information had been transmitted to the department by the Spanish Ambassador without explanation.

The *Chronicle* made a scoop. What would you have deduced from the situation?

The questions to be answered are:

1. *What had Trimpi done that caused his arrest?* (Credit 5.)

2. *What was the gist of the* Chronicle's *scoop?* (Credit 5.)

Credit Score:

NO. 10

THE CLUB CAR MYSTERY AT SYRACUSE

There are times in the solution of practical mysteries when quick thinking is essential. Only the failure to think and act quickly in the celebrated Cleveland–New York express train affair (on the part of the detectives in that case) is responsible for the incident going down in history as an unsolved mystery. At least that is the opinion of Captain McCumber of the Syracuse Police, who furnishes the following facts established by that ill-managed investigation, to which, unfortunately, he was summoned so late.

THE CLEVELAND–NEW YORK EXPRESS on the night of March 23, 1925, was fifteen minutes late on its run from Rochester east into Syracuse. It was, therefore, speeding to make up time. There were unusually few passengers aboard. At the last call for dinner, which was made by a dining-car waiter at 7:40, the club car on the rear end of the train was virtually, if not entirely, deserted by passengers for the diner forward. There was no specific testimony on this point from anyone in the entire course of the investigation.

At about 7:50 William Osborne, a realtor of Cleveland, passenger on the train, finished his dinner and returned to the club car, where he had spent the afternoon, to smoke a cigar. Osborne's testimony, subsequently given to the detectives, was as follows:

I tried the door leading into the club car, and it was locked. I banged on the door, hoping to attract the porter's attention; then I saw a bell near the door and rang that hard several times. Then I pounded loud. Pretty soon the brakeman, or maybe it was one of the conductors, peeked out from behind the curtain of the window in the door, and then he opened the door a little bit. I don't remember what he looked like, only that he was white, not a Negro, and he was in uniform.

"Car is closed," he said; "something's the matter with this car – just wait a few minutes until we get it fixed."

"All right," I said, as he was starting to close the door on me, "but please give me the right railroad time, will you? My watch has stopped."

I noticed he was kind of impatient, but he pulled out his watch and said:

"Eight of eight."

I set my watch and turned back, and I guess he locked the door again, but I didn't notice. I never thought anything of it. Then I went back in the next Pullman in front and sat down.

Asked by a detective: "Are you sure he said 'eight of eight'?" Osborne replied in the affirmative. He remembered it distinctly, he said, because the repetition struck his ear.

According to further testimony of Osborne, approximately two or three minutes later the train slowed down perceptibly on approaching the railroad yard at Syracuse, and a minute or so later had slackened its speed even more as it entered the yards.

At 7:55 Pullman Conductor Yeats and Train Conductor Sedgwick, who had been chatting with passengers forward since 7:30, passed through the train toward the rear and were surprised to discover the club car locked. Thinking that the Pullman porter possibly was taking an opportunity to serve liquor to passengers on the sly, the Pullman conductor opened the door with his key and strode forward with a rebuke on his lips. He stumbled over the crumpled figure of Arthur Johnson, the colored porter, whose head was bleeding from a cut at the back. The porter was unconscious on the floor near the door. He did not respond to ice water dashed in his face.

The conductors rushed forward. To their amazement the club car was deserted. Not a person was to be seen. They hurried to the back platform in search of Dennis Sloan, the brakeman. But Sloan was not there as he should have been.

Had he fallen off? Both conductors strained their eyes back over the receding tracks but could discern no trace of anyone having fallen off the train. They rushed through the train searching for Sloan everywhere. He was not on the train. Even the car roofs were searched in vain.

When Pullman Conductor Yeats had first entered the car and discovered the unconscious porter, Train Conductor Sedgwick had examined the lavatory at the front end of the club car and found it empty. Indeed, all facts of the investigation subsequently established that no one had left the club car *after* the two conductors had entered it.

The conductors were at an absolute loss to explain the situation. Sloan, the young brakeman, had been a trustworthy and exemplary employee for more than three years. Had he and the porter quarreled? Had they come to blows, and had Sloan fled upon discov-

ering that a blow had rendered the porter unconscious? They had been, apparently, on most amicable
terms during the afternoon. Why had the brakeman
deserted his post? No attempt had been made to rob
the porter of money, but his keys were missing.

As the train pulled into the Syracuse station, Pullman Conductor Yeats discovered the missing brakeman's visored cap and blue-cloth, brass-buttoned
coat, neatly rolled into a ball, jammed into the drawer
of the writing desk at the rear end of the club car!

The city detective on duty in the station conferred
with the conductors. William Osborne, the passenger,
heard of the excitement and came forward then with
his testimony.

It was at this juncture that the station master hurried up with a telegram just received from the railroad's agent at Ford's Crossing, a hamlet twelve miles
west of Syracuse on the railroad line. It said:

Westbound Number 47 stopped one-quarter
mile west of here to avoid running over body on
westbound tracks. Man dead. Revolver bullet
hole behind left ear. Description, six feet one,
about two hundred pounds, age about sixty,
gray moustache, well dressed, brown tweed suit,
wallet containing three hundred fifty dollars
and commutation ticket Long Island Railroad

between Hempstead and New York City, in name of Anthony Capewell. Wallet initials J. A. C. Was he dropped from Number Thirty-one? Local constable in charge. Instruct me.

MURTREE, Agent.

Train Number 31 was the Cleveland–New York express.

You have now all the facts of the mystery which confronted the detectives in the Syracuse station upon the arrival of the train.

None of the passengers or train crew could add anything to the meager data available. Doctors in care of Johnson, the Pullman porter, feared that he might not regain consciousness for several hours. Yet the need for immediate action was obvious.

Suppose you had been in charge of the investigation – what would you have deduced about the mystery? How would you have reasoned and acted in the emergency?

These are the questions to be answered:

1. *What would you have done to locate Dennis Sloan, the brakeman?* (Credit 3.)

2. *Would you have ordered the arrest of Dennis Sloan, the brakeman, on a charge of murder of Capewell?*
(Credit 2.)

3. *Would you have ordered his arrest as an accomplice?*
(Credit 1.)

4. *Was Sloan guilty of assault on the porter?* (Credit 2.)

5. *What in all probability happened in the club car after the last call to dinner?* (Credit 2.)

Credit Score:

NO. II

THE MYSTERY OF
HAJI LAL DEB

No land offers more bizarre and ingenious crimes and con-cealments of crimes than India. Naturally subtle, the Ori-ental mind, when it does turn to crime, manages sometimes to baffle the authorities rather neatly. Until as late as 1880 British rule in India had not become adept in fighting the elaborate system of highway robbery gang thieving (dacoity), *and professional poisoning which had been spreading virtually unchecked for many years. British detectives in the Indian service were confronted with strange conditions among strange peoples. Gradually they learned how to cope with Indian crime.*

The following problem in crime detection is based on an extract from the case book of Deputy Superintendent Hardesty Mainwaring of the Bombay district, who later rose to head the Metropolitan Police of London. In his Looking Backward (*Methuen, Ltd., London, 1905*)*, the famous investigator writes:*

LATE IN THE SUMMER of 1879, shortly after my first colonial appointment, I was requested by the native officer at Bunoorah to advise on a baffling case which was arousing considerable excitement in that village.

Some ten days previously a well-to-do merchant of the village had vanished mysteriously one night when he was known to be carrying a sizeable sum in rupees. No word having come from him the morning after his disappearance, the merchant's widow had raised a hue and cry with the local authorities. There was some reason to suspect that the man had been done away with, for murder to gain a few rupees was common enough at that time – and the merchant was a tempting bait to the professional poisoners operating in the district.

Among others upon whom a certain measure of suspicion rested was a former servant in the household of the merchant, one Haji Lal Deb. Several months previously he had been discharged on suspicion of stealing foodstuffs, and although the authorities had nothing definite to go on they instinctively had reached the conclusion that Haji Lal Deb knew something of the matter.

However, "knowing" and "proving" in India are two very different things. The former servant was a stone wall when it came to giving information as to the whereabouts of the merchant. He convinced the native officer that he had not the slightest idea of what could have happened in the affair. No less than seven relatives and friends staunchly supported his statements, and nothing came of the questioning. Nor were the authorities more successful in their quest at other sources.

But on the day of my arrival at Bunoorah – some two weeks after the disappearance – a native woman of the village came to the local investigating officer with the following story. She assigned as her reason for not having come sooner that she had been ill and had heard nothing of the gossip of the disappearance.

Very early in the morning of the day following the disappearance of the merchant, she recalled, she had encountered Haji Lal Deb walking rapidly away from a certain isolated district on the outskirts of the town *carrying a spade over his shoulder*. She was in a hurry herself to visit her brother, who was ill of the plague then afflicting the district, and had thought nothing of the incident. Haji Lal Deb, she remembered, was walking toward his hut, which was itself on the outskirts of the village.

With something of a gleam of triumph in our eyes, the local investigating officer and I proceeded immediately to the hut and there found Haji Lal Deb – as calm, impassive, and innocent looking an old native as you could imagine.

To our amazement he admitted readily enough that he had been walking in the spot described at the time described, and carrying a spade. But he knew nothing of the rich merchant, said he; he had been engaged on the sad errand of burying his wife's cousin, an aged man who had died of the plague the night previous. And would Sahib not believe him? Come, he would show Sahib the very grave.

Now it was perfectly true that the fellow might be telling the truth. The natives had been dying off like flies at this time, and there was nothing unusual about a hurried burial of a body, under the emergency conditions then obtaining. Indeed to prevent spread of the disease, prompt burial would have been essential. The native officer recalled the report that a relative in the house of Haji Lal Deb had died about the time of the disappearance of the merchant, and he duly noted that the household had engaged in observance of suitable rites of mourning.

However, it seemed the part of prudence to check the story, and accordingly we allowed Haji Lal Deb to lead us to the spot where the aged relative had been buried. To our astonishment – for I had come to suspect the fellow – our spadesmen had not dug more than three feet down when we came upon the body of an aged native. Most evidently he had died of the plague, and there could be no mistaking that it was the corpse of an old, emaciated man, whereas the missing merchant had been a stout fellow in the prime of life.

I had never felt more "sold" in my life. The local officer and I were indeed so moved that we pressed a few rupees on Haji Lal Deb, and with some words of apology retired to seek solution of the mystery elsewhere.

There were some trifling clues which we thought might lead somewhere along other trails, and we were engaged in sifting these in their possible relation to other suspects when suddenly we received a bit of information which I recognized as of the greatest importance. It was given to us by the son of a neighbor of Haji Lal Deb who happened to overhear us lamenting the fruitlessness of our expedition of the morning.

The aged cousin of the wife of Haji Lal Deb, we learned, had died the day *before* the disappearance of the merchant, not *on* the night of the disappearance. . . .

How Deputy Superintendent Mainwaring solved the mystery and fastened the guilt upon Haji Lal Deb is one of the classics of crime detection in the Bombay district.

The questions to be answered are:

1. *Why did Mainwaring suspect that Haji was guilty?* (Credit 4.)

2. *By what step did he prove the guilt?* (Credit 6.)

Credit Score:

NO. 12

THE STRANGE CASE OF THE PROMISSORY NOTE

WHEN RICHARD MANNINGTON died in 1902 he left to his widow a fortune of $1,200,000 and his famous collection of porcelains. Scarcely ten days after Mannington's death the widow received a bombshell in the form of the following letter from one Philip Renoir of San Francisco:

> At this time of your sorrow, I hesitate to speak of a matter which goes back more than twenty years, when your late husband and I had our unfortunate disagreement over the Ming vases, of the details of which you are undoubtedly to some extent aware. I had thought never to be obliged to advance my claim, but circumstances now compel it in justice to myself and others.
>
> In June, 1882, I had just returned from a five

74

years' stay in China, when I became acquainted with your husband at the home of the Levericks in Washington Square. I had brought with me seventeen pieces, including the two vases of the Ming Dynasty, which to-day form the basis of your late husband's celebrated collection. Mannington was at that time interested more as a speculator, attracted by the chance of profit in the purchase and sale of Chinese art, than he was in collecting for art's sake. To make a long story short, he purchased from me at that time the pieces enumerated upon the attached separate memorandum, and at the prices named. He paid me then, according to our agreement, $5,000 in cash, and gave me his promissory note for $32,000, $37,000 being the total amount of the transaction.

It is one of the regrets of my life that out of this transaction grew the serious misunderstanding between us which resulted a year later in a rupture of our friendly relations. You probably are aware that soon after the making of our agreement several experts, undoubtedly bribed by envious dealers, declared the vases counterfeit. Your husband ultimately refused point-blank to pay his note.

Perhaps you are *not* aware that after violent

disputes on the matter the authenticity of the pieces was established beyond a doubt only six months ago. Until this had occurred I did not care to press my claim against your husband, although personally I had never doubted that the vases were genuine. I had written several times to your husband since then but received no reply whatever. Three months ago I was on the point of bringing suit against him when I was taken seriously ill, an illness from which I have only just recovered.

I repeat that it gives me pain to force the issue at this time, but circumstances compel me to do so. I am sure we both wish to avoid the unpleasantness of a suit, and I have determined to throw myself upon your sense of justice, even though the technicalities of the law might seem to make recognition of the debt unlikely in view of the lapse of years.

I enclose a photostatic copy of your husband's note. The original is in the possession of my attorneys, McArthur, Longon & McArthur, First National Bank Building, San Francisco, from whom any further details may be had. I trust, however, that we may settle the matter between ourselves rather than between attorneys.

Mrs. Mannington had been married to her husband for only ten years. He was a man who had never discussed business matters with his wife, and she could neither deny nor affirm the justice of the claim. The note, according to what was said to be a photostatic copy of it, bore Mannington's distinctive signature. The formal text of the note, duly couched in the correct legal language, was typewritten. It was turned over to handwriting and typewriting experts, who pronounced it authentic. The handwriting experts, and some of Mannington's old friends, advised the widow that the signature was not only undoubtedly that of Mannington but that it was characteristic of Mannington's signature at that particular period of his life. And the typewriting experts pronounced the type characteristic of the machines used in the early 'eighties.

No record of the transaction could be found in the papers of the deceased, but the details regarding the authentication of the Ming jars proved to be true. A complete report of the authentication had recently been published by the *Ceramics Journal*. Of Philip Renoir, the claimant, Mrs. Mannington knew only that he had indeed been an old friend of her late husband, and that Renoir was the brother of Adèle Renoir, now deceased, who had been a sweetheart of Mannington in the early 'eighties. It was known that Adèle Renoir and Mannington had once carried on an extensive correspondence.

This was not the first time that Mrs. Mannington's faith in her late husband's integrity had been disturbed. Before her marriage she had heard ugly gossip of the methods by which he had gained his fortune. She knew that throughout her married life he had been almost jealously devoted to his valuable collection. Had he in his earlier years stooped to dishonesty in assembling it? To her any threat of stain on her dead husband's reputation was terrifying. Anxious to avoid publicity she directed her attorney to accompany her to San Francisco to examine the original document and settle the matter at once.

At the ensuing conference with Renoir and his lawyers, Mrs. Mannington and her attorney were favorably impressed by the claimant. Philip Renoir was a large, suave, courtly gentleman, apparently of the greatest sincerity. His attorneys were among the best known in the city, and had been established for years. The original note, slightly yellowed with age, was produced. Mrs. Mannington and her lawyer compared it carefully with the photostatic copy which had been sent to them. They were obviously identical.

Anxious to settle the matter and feeling financially able to do so, the widow announced frankly her willingness to take up the note. Everyone was pleased. The lady was about to draw the check, and the lawyers were congratulating each other upon the happy settlement of the affair, when suddenly Mrs. Mannington's eyes fell upon the back of the note which bore her husband's signature.

She paused and asked to examine the document again. Renoir's lawyer handed it to her.

It was about six inches wide and a little less from top to bottom. Mannington's signature, directly under the typed lines of the promise to pay, fell in the center of the paper (from side to side), a quarter of an inch above the bottom edge of the paper.

Turning the note over, Mrs. Mannington examined what had caught her eye on the back. This is what she saw along the bottom margin in a spot almost coinciding with the signature on the reverse of the sheet:

These lines, obviously made by pen and ink, were the only markings on the back of the note.

Mrs. Mannington looked at them carelessly and handed the note back. She then said she had not brought the right check book with her and would have to return to her hotel and get it. She departed with her lawyer at 5 P.M. But she never returned.

Early that evening Mrs. Mannington's lawyer called on Mr. McArthur, senior member of the firm of lawyers representing Renoir, and warned him that Philip Renoir was in all probability a clever crook. Shocked, Mr. McArthur demanded the reasons for the charge, and when he heard them he paused in dismay. In the presence of the Mannington lawyer he telephoned to Renoir's residential hotel.

"Mr. Renoir was called out of town suddenly just before supper," he was informed by the hotel clerk.

And San Francisco never heard of Philip Renoir again.

What had aroused Mrs. Mannington's suspicions and what had Renoir done? Had you been a detective assigned to the case, what would you have made of the mystery?

The questions to be answered are:

1. *Why did the strange markings on the back of the yellowed document lead Mrs. Mannington to suspect that something might be wrong?* (Credit 3.)

2. *Where had Renoir probably obtained the piece of paper which bore Mannington's signature?* (Credit 7.)

Credit Score:

NO. 13

THE DEATH OF
BARNABAS FROBISHER

Barnabas Frobisher, retired automobile manufacturer, was found dead in his library, a bullet through his head. Had a crime been committed? If so, by whom and how? Answers to these questions can be deduced from the following established facts and the official police sketch of the death scene.

AT 9:25 ON THE EVENING of January 12th the police received a telephone call from a man who spoke in an excited voice:

"This is the butler at Barnabas Frobisher's. Mr. Frobisher has shot himself. He's just killed himself. I'm all alone in the house. It's terrible. What? 230 Sandhurst Avenue. Yes, I'll stay right here. Graves – John Graves, the butler."

The police found Graves and Annie O'Hagen, the cook, who had just come in, waiting anxiously by the front door. In the library they found Barnabas

Frobisher slumped down in an armchair, dead from a bullet which had entered the middle of his forehead. A revolver, later identified as Frobisher's, lay on the seat of the chair between the side of the chair and the left thigh of the dead man, as it might have fallen if it had slipped from his grasp. Below the wound and on the backs of the fingers of both hands were powder marks. On the revolver were faint traces of finger prints which were later found to be Frobisher's. Only one bullet had been fired from the revolver and it was this bullet which had killed Frobisher. The body had not been robbed.

Pending the arrival of Frobisher's wife, who had been summoned from her box at the opera, the police examined the butler and the cook. The butler told the following story:

It is no secret that Mr. Frobisher has been losing money from speculations lately. He has not been himself. He has quarreled with his wife several times in the last few weeks over what he called her extravagances. She denounced him for speculating, and they did not speak to each other for the last twenty minutes of dinner.

Mrs. Frobisher went to the opera at 8:10, and Mr. Frobisher went into the library a couple of minutes later and locked the door after him, as he usually does. I took him his port as soon as he went in, and I came right out. Then I stayed in the pantry and the kitchen waiting if he should call for anything, and at about nine o'clock the cook left the kitchen to go to the fire down the street. I heard the fire engines making a loud noise off and on for the next fifteen or twenty minutes. Then it suddenly occurred to me that maybe Mr. Frobisher had rung and that I hadn't heard it. The buzzer sounds in the pantry, and I had been listening to the fire commotion from the back kitchen window. So I went into the pantry and knocked on the door to the library. There was no answer. I opened it a little and I saw him slumped down just as you found him, with his head all bleeding. I rushed in and felt his pulse and saw he was dead, and went right out without touching a thing, and telephoned to the police station. That is all I know. He must have shot himself while the fire engines were going by and I didn't hear the shot.

Annie O'Hagen, the old and trusted cook of the Frobisher household, corroborated the butler's presence in the pantry and kitchen until about 9 o'clock. It was established that Frobisher was alive at about nine o'clock, for before leaving for the fire the cook, stopping in the pantry, heard him cough in the adjacent

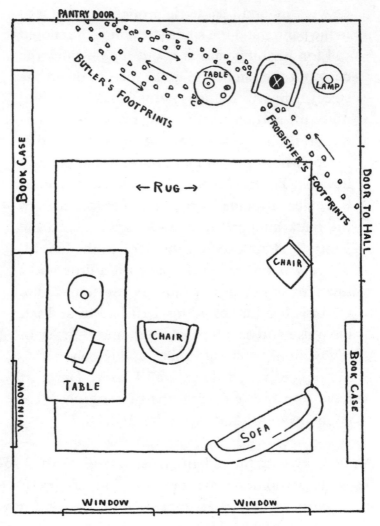

Diagram of the Frobisher library.

library, and heard his glass laid down on the taboret. The butler, she testified, was at that time in the kitchen. She then heard the fire sirens and rushed out, telling the butler that she might be away a half hour if the blaze was an exciting one. Ten minutes later a second alarm was turned in and more fire engines passed the house. When the cook returned at 9:25, she overheard the ending of the butler's telephone conversation with the police station.

Was the butler telling the truth? The police examined minutely the highly polished surface of the newly waxed floor of the library and found there what seemed to be corroboration of his story. Frobisher's heel marks from the door connecting to the hall led to the armchair in which he was found – and ended there. It was established that he customarily went to the library after dinner, bolted the door after him to prevent disturbance, and often sat there reading for hours. The door was found bolted by the police.

From the door between pantry and library were two coming and two going sets of heel marks which fitted the butler's shoes. They agreed with his statement of his only two trips into the room: first, to serve the wine; later, to examine the body. Careful examination of the floor revealed no other footprints but the detectives, by tests, determined that a person might have walked in stockinged feet on the floor without leaving any mark. Only the rubber heels, worn by both Frobisher and the butler, had left prints.

Mrs. Frobisher, arriving on the scene, confirmed the butler's testimony of quarrels over speculation with her husband, but denied vehemently that he would have taken his own life merely on that account or because of losses from speculations. She said she could offer no adequate reason for suicide. On the other hand, she could not suggest why anyone should have desired his death. She testified most positively – and her opinion was shared by the cook – that Frobisher was the kind of man who would not commit suicide. On the other hand, both refused to believe that John Graves, the butler, could have shot Frobisher, for neither knew of any animosity between the two men or any possible motive. Graves had been with the family for only two months.

Investigation revealed that Mrs. Frobisher had been at the opera from 8:25 until summoned home by the tragedy, and that Annie O'Hagen had been at the fire during the time she had said she was there. John Graves, the butler, stoutly denied further knowledge. When asked if he thought it possible that some intruder had entered the house and shot Frobisher while he, Graves, was in the kitchen, the butler denied the possibility. He pointed out that the hall door of the library and all the windows had been locked from the inside. The police had found this to be the case.

You now have all the evidence which was available to the police on the night of the death of Barnabas Frobisher. What do you deduce about the mystery? Three days later much light was shed by the discovery of certain papers in the private files of the dead man, and of these you will read in the Answer Section. Meanwhile, these are the questions to be answered:

1. *At whose hands did Barnabas Frobisher meet his death?* (Credit 5.)

2. *How do you know it?* (Credit 5.)

Credit Score:

NO. 14

THE PROBLEM OF THE AMNESIA CASE

Could you have solved the problem which confronted the police of Birmingham in 1922?

ON HIS ROUNDS through a park in the city of Birmingham, England, a policeman found a man in a badly dazed condition. When asked who he was and where he came from, his replies were incoherent. He was taken to the police station and later lodged in a hospital. Here they judged from his clothing that he was an American, but found no way of determining his identity or any clues to his friends or relatives until he began to talk. It was an amnesia case. A record was kept of his remarks. Among these were:

> Don't keep bothering about me – it's thirty for me and I know it. . . . I can't seem to remember much of anything, but what does that matter? It's thirty now. . . .

They always made you say it was a fire. But everybody knew different. "What *started* the fire?" (And here the amnesia victim laughed loudly.)

We only had three trunks then – three trunks for the whole push. We were all working emergency then. . . . But it's thirty for me now.

None of the doctors, nurses, or policemen who had been assigned to the case from time to time could make anything out of it. But it happened that one member of the force, who had lived extensively in America, returned one day from London, where he had been assigned to a case. He examined the remarks and quickly deduced where the unfortunate man had worked at one time in the United States, and his probable line of work. Through his deductions the Birmingham police were able to communicate with those who could come to the amnesia victim's assistance.

The questions to be answered are:

1. *In what city had the amnesia victim once worked?* (Credit 7.)

2. *What probably had been his line of work?* (Credit 3.)

Credit Score:

NO. 15

THE HUPPENHEIMER MUSEUM ROBBERY

This is a long and complicated mystery. Read it carefully.

ONE SUNDAY MORNING, soon after the great Huppenheimer Museum of Pittsburgh had opened its doors for the day, a guard on the second floor was startled by a ponderous clank from a corridor in the Egyptian wing. Thinking that a statue had fallen, he rushed in the direction of the sound. Instead he saw a man, who was struggling to replace the heavy lid of a sarcophagus, suddenly let go of the lid and dart away. The guard seized his coat collar, but the fugitive squirmed from his coat, dodged behind an exhibit case, and vanished. When the breathless guard arrived downstairs at the front door he found that the intruder had walked out quietly and was lost from sight. The doorman had supposed him a workman of the museum and had thought nothing of his departure.

This event brought to the attention of the authorities the singular incident of the museum robbery which resulted in the great scandal of 1924. Detective Wagner, who was assigned to the case, later summarized the affair as follows:

I arrived at the museum Monday morning and was ushered into the office of Director Oddie, who had the captured coat on a chair beside him. The doctor told me of the coat incident and then said:

"I am sorry to say that this means a clever attempt at a serious robbery. This fellow to whom the coat belongs had undoubtedly managed to stay in the museum overnight. Investigation revealed that our case number 12 had been robbed of its contents in a most ingenious manner. But fortunately the thief has been badly fooled. What he was after, of course, was the Rurik gem collection which Mr. Huppenheimer purchased only last year. What he got was the set of paste replicas which we always keep in the exhibit case except upon occasions when distinguished persons visit us. The real gems are then taken from a safe and temporarily installed in the case. Now, this fellow had cunningly prepared a dummy set of the gems, in their distinctive settings, and had managed to insert them in the case when he extracted what he thought were the real jewels.

"In short, we have played an $80,000 joke on the robber. At the same time, I shudder at the ease with which the fellow did his work. It is of the utmost importance, of course, that we track the man down.

"This may not be so hard as you think"; Dr. Oddie continued, "for I learned this morning from Curator Waltham, of the Section of Antique Jewels, that the owner of the coat has probably been in the museum frequently in the last few weeks. Three weeks ago to-morrow a man representing himself as Antonio Diaz, a designer of jewelry, applied for permission to make drawings of the Rurik pieces. The copying of designs by the public, you know, is a regular thing with us. We encourage it to aid all the industrial arts and handicrafts. Persons have frequently copied the Rurik designs. They have to do this through the glass of the case, using a magnifying glass.

"Our guard is always near the case in the daytime. The thief could not have taken the screws out of the case except by night. This he did, removing the paste replicas and substituting the fake pieces which he had made. As you will see, the dummy set is cleverly made. The fellow had not spent his days of copying for nothing. He hoped, of course, to make his way out of the museum in the morning with what he thought was the real set, leaving his dummy set to lull us into continued security.

"Indeed, had he not replaced several of the screws crookedly, I doubt if we would have noticed which case had been tampered with. Our night watchman makes the rounds every half hour; the thief must have been hurried as he was finishing his task of screwing up the side of the case. The culprit, I take it, must have hidden in the sarcophagus during the early hours of light Sunday morning, while waiting for the doors to open. He would have escaped without leaving any clue whatever if the guard in the Egyptian wing had not seen him. Probably while climbing out of the sarcophagus the lid slipped from his grasp. Now the question is: what does this coat tell you?"

And Dr. Oddie handed it to me.

I examined the coat and the contents of its pockets, but had to confess to Dr. Oddie that I could make nothing of it. It was an ordinary brown coat of cheviot, well worn. There was no label or identifying mark of any kind. The right-hand pocket yielded a cheap screwdriver and a piece of white string. In the left-hand pocket we found a small gimlet, some rubber bands, and a package of wintergreen drops. In the upper left-hand pocket (outside breast) I found two stubs of tickets to a large New York movie theater – very much frayed, and a bit of white paper about three inches by one. This was not soiled or frayed, as were the ticket stubs. I judged that it was a portion of a roll from an adding machine, for it had printed on it a column of numbers, as if someone had started to add a series of checks or amount of money. No total, however, was given. It ran thus:

```
12.09
23.22
 9.22
23.13
27.18
15.15
76.22
 8.23
26.28
79.18
16.22
 8.12
12.13
```

I was about to request Dr. Oddie to take me to case number 12 for a search for fingerprints when the door of the office burst open and a tall, elderly man rushed in on us in the greatest excitement.

"Doctor!" he cried, "we have been robbed. It is terrible! The pieces in the safe are not the originals! A terrible mistake must have been made, and the thief has taken the *real* gems."

It was Curator Waltham, who had just come from the safe where the real jewels supposedly were resting. Dr. Oddie and I were staggered at this turn of events. We hastily plied the curator for details.

Three weeks ago to the day, Curator Waltham said, he personally had removed the real gems from the safe and examined them carefully in anticipation of their exhibit to the Prince of Wales, who was to visit the museum that noon. To make way for them he had directed Assistant Curator Raymond to remove the replicas from the case (number 12) and keep them in his desk.

The curator testified in the most absolute way that he personally had carried the real gems to the case and had himself installed them there. He remained while the guards locked the case before his eyes, and stood directly by the case awaiting the reception committee and the Prince.

Only the curator had the key to the lock. He was prepared, if the Prince expressed a desire to handle the famous pieces, to remove them himself and hand them to the Prince. However, the visit was hurried, and the Prince did not make the request.

Of the subsequent events Curator Waltham said:

"I remember distinctly that after the Prince left, I left Assistant Curator Raymond in charge to remove the true pieces and put them securely away in the safe, for I was compelled to join the committee accompanying His Highness for the rest of the tour through the museum. I cannot say that I saw Raymond do it, but I am as certain of his honor and integrity as I am of my own. He reported to me only an hour later that he had done so, and that the paste replicas had been restored to case number 12.

"Yet Raymond is so careful, it seems impossible that he could have made any mistake about this. I confess that I am inclined to the belief that this thief whose coat was captured in some way must have obtained the combination of the safe and stolen the real pieces from *it*, also robbing the case of the replicas and putting them in the safe. Thus he hoped that a long time would elapse before the fraud would be discovered in either safe or exhibit case, since our replicas would be in the safe and his dummy set in the case. That would give him more time to sell them without an alarm being spread."

Dr. Oddie affirmed in the most positive manner his complete trust in both the Curator and the Assistant Curator. He added that he agreed with Curator Waltham's theory. However, they placed the investigation entirely in my hands and were good enough to express the fullest confidence in me.

Our first step was to telegraph Mr. Raymond, the Assistant Curator, recalling him immediately from an emergency mission to the New York Metropolitan Museum of Art, on which he had been sent the Friday before. Within a few hours Raymond had wired that he was starting back at once.

In the meantime I made a searching investigation among this Raymond's friends, and found that he bore a reputation for good character and devotion to the museum. He arrived the next day.

I would describe him as a scholarly appearing young man in his early thirties, with a frank, open countenance, though highly nervous in his manner. He appeared to be greatly shocked at what had taken place, immediately offered to resign, and courted the fullest investigation.

He told us convincingly that he personally had removed the jewels from the case. Then, he said, he had put them into the safe and locked it; after which he had carried the replicas from his desk back to case number 12 and inserted them in their proper places. He had personally supervised the locking of the case and examined it to see if it was secured – all before he had gone to luncheon on the day of the visit of the Prince.

I confess that I was persuaded as to his sincerity and the truth of his story, as were Dr. Oddie and Curator Waltham. I was completely baffled. I had been unable to get any trace of Antonio Diaz (no doubt an alias) and after several days' searching my investigation left me as mystified as ever.

There were no fingerprints on the case or on the museum safe. None of the guards could shed light on the mystery. I was certain that it was an inside job, but I couldn't lay finger on a person. Only Dr. Oddie, Curator Waltham and

Assistant Curator Raymond possessed the combination of the safe which had held the jewels.

Such was Detective Wagner's summary of the case up to the evening of March 3rd. On that evening, as he was sitting in his office in Police Headquarters, reexamining the captured coat and its contents, an idea occurred to him. By dawn he had reached a solution of the mystery.

It was as clever a piece of detective work as the country had seen in twenty years. Before noon of that day a man had been arrested on the charge of robbing the Huppenheimer Museum. Who was that man? How did the detective know it? What would you have deduced?

The questions to be answered are:

1. *How many were guilty in the robbery?* (Credit 2.)

2. *Who?* (Credit 3.)

3. *How was the robbery carried out?* (Credit 2.)

4. How was the guilt conclusively proved? (Credit 3.)

Credit Score:

A NOTE ON THE TYPE

The Baffle Book has been set in Plantin, a face cut for Monotype in 1913 under the direction of Frank Hinman Pierpont. The fruit of Pierpont's research in the collection of the Plantin-Moretus Museum in Antwerp, Plantin is based on types cut in the sixteenth century by the peripatetic French typographer Robert Granjon. Unlike the more studious revivals released during Stanley Morison's tenure at Monotype, Plantin was freely adapted to the demands of modern printing: its strokes were thickened and its descenders shortened, making it a popular type for printers of periodicals. In fact, Plantin was so successful in this realm that it would later serve as one of the models for Morison's own Times New Roman. A face of considerable heft and warmth, Plantin was particularly popular among European printers and was one of the first types to be adapted for use in offset lithography.

*　　*
*

Design and composition by
Carl W. Scarbrough

ANSWER SECTION

The Problem of Napoleon's Signatures

1. The signature as General in Chief of the Egyptian Expedition was B: "Bonaparte." This was done in 1798 when Bonaparte was only twenty-nine years old. He had been successful as a soldier but his character had not formed as in the signature of 1806 (D). The unsettled or unformed nature of the writing (compared with D) and the fact that he signed "Bonaparte" instead of "Napoleon" should indicate the identity of the signature. (Credit 2.)

2. The signature when he first became Emperor in 1804 was H. This is written "Napoleon" (he chose to become known as Napoleon I). It resembles somewhat B. He had not yet developed the complete mastery of himself that is to be seen in D (1806). (Credit 3.)

3. The signature at Tilsit was G: a mere "N." It is sweeping, triumphant, masterful. This was in 1807. Compare with the indecision of F signature (six years later) when his defeat was threatened. (Credit 2.)

4. The signature at Elba was C. It shows clearly the breaking down of the man and his fortunes, yet it has some dash. It lacks the resignation of the St. Helena signature, E. (Credit 2.)

5. The St. Helena signature is E – note how the

3

B

Written as Chief of the Egyptian Expedition in 1798.

H

Done very soon after becoming Emperor, in 1804. Age 35.

D

Done at Berlin, October 29, 1806. At the very height of his career.
He was still thinking clearly. Egotism had not yet dominated.

G

At the Imperial Camp at Tilsit, 1807, when the Emperor had virtually all
Europe, except England, at his mercy. Perhaps the climax of his military
successes, but the beginning of his tremendous egotism.

F

Done October 1, 1813. Bonaparte's enemies were slowly but surely wearing him down. Several of his armies commanded by his marshals had been defeated. Yet he was not to be beaten decisively until 1815.

A

A few days before his abdication as Emperor (just before voluntary exile on Elba). Done April 4, 1814.

C

September, 1814. From the island of Elba.

E

Done two months after arriving at St. Helena on his forced and final exile. Date December, 1816.

capital N has slumped down almost to the level of the smaller letters. Compare it with the virility of the D signature, which was done ten years before. (Credit 1.)

The various signatures, in their chronological order, on preceding pages tell a rather obvious story of the rise and fall of Napoleon Bonaparte.

No. 2
THE GREAT IMPERIAL BANK ROBBERY

1. The tire tracks which at first baffled Elkins were clearly those of an aëroplane.

The robbers had confederates in an aëroplane circling over the road to Derham, waiting for their car. When the pilot caught sight of the car, perhaps identifying it through some prearranged signal, he came down and landed in the road some distance in front of it. The car then came up behind, and the robbers transferred the loot, their guns, and the clothes in which they had committed the robbery into the aëroplane. The width between the tire tracks compared with the width of the automobile tracks indicate an aëroplane. The narrow tires, without markings, and the mid-track made by the metal tail skid of the machine, are also characteristic. (Credit 7.)

6

2. A detective would in all probability radio a general alarm for aëroplanes seen anywhere in the vicinity, try to learn the direction each had taken, where it had landed, and make a thorough check-up of all such machines. (Credit 3.)

No. 3
THE PROBLEM AT THE ABANDONED BUNGALOW

1. In all probability there were four men in the gang at the abandoned bungalow. This is indicated by the number of cups, and by other clues which follow. (Credit 2.)

2. The man who sat in the chair in the right foreground of the illustration was probably a tall man with a sore or wounded foot. From the illustration it will be seen that the chair on which the bottle of iodine stands is in a direct line with this chair, and from the direction in which the latter chair is turned it is possible to deduce that the man who sat in it was using the other chair as a foot rest. The chairs were not very near together, so the police deduced that it was a *tall* man who had the sore foot. Probably his neighbor at the left had been dressing the wound for him and had placed the iodine on the nearest edge of the chair used for a foot rest.

This man to the left must have been a pipe smoker, judging from the large number of burned *wooden* matches around his chair. Many pipe smokers prefer the larger and longer burning flame of wooden matches to the short-lived paper ones.

The man in back of the table (in the illustration) was evidently left-handed, as is indicated by the position of his cup with relation to his chair.

The man who sat on the wooden box and drummed with his heels, making the dents in the box, was an unusually short man, or at least had very short legs, as shown by the distance of the dents from the top of the box. He probably was short in the trunk also, as he evidently chose the high wooden box to sit on. The cigar butt found by the cup at this place indicated almost certainly that the short one was not a woman. (Credit 8.)

No. 4
THE WARFIELD–COBHAM JEWEL ROBBERY

1. The butler was an accomplice in the Warfield-Cobham jewel robbery. (Credit 1.)

2. The advertisement which the detective took from the "Situations Wanted, Male" column was really a message in cipher. Taking every sixth word in the advertisement, the message reads:

Back bureau northwest second business offers opportunity Wednesday twelve.

Answer Section

The detective saw that this message constituted directions for robbing Mrs. Warfield-Cobham's home. "Back bureau" obviously meant "back of the bureau," the location of the wall safe in the widow's bedroom. "Northwest second" must have referred to the location of the room, which was the northwest room on the second floor. The rest of the message indicated that Wednesday midnight would be a favorable time. (Credit 9.)

Ardmore was arrested that night at the Warfield-Cobham home, and "Gentleman Claude" was caught two weeks later in Kansas City. Both men were convicted and given long sentences. As to his reasons for employing the devious method of communication with his confederate, Ardmore later explained as follows to the police:

"It wasn't my idea, but Claude was afraid to call for mail anywhere, and he feared that a telephone or telegraph message from the house would be traced to me. I never thought of doing anything like this, but Claude had heard about the stuff [the jewels] being bought, and he said he could handle the job alone if I would just tip him off and let him in."

Ardmore had had a good record, according to the police, until he had fallen under the influence of "Gentleman Claude" a year previously. The use of the newspaper want advertisement as a cipher appealed to the Canadian criminal as safe and amusing.

No. 5
THE LA JOYA RIVER HOMICIDE

1. Search for further clues should have been directed to the Gordon Ranch. (Credit 10.)

Since the victim had been strangled before immersion, his body may have assumed to have floated and drifted with the current on the east side of the river, which ran at a speed of six miles per hour. Since the hands of the watch, when examined, pointed to 5:25 (and it had been recently wound up and therefore had been running); and since the immersion tests with similar watches indicated that the water caused it to stop within two to four minutes, the time of the body striking the water may be assumed to be about 5:21 or 5:23.

The body was sighted going over the mill dam at 6:13. It had therefore been floating down for fifty or fifty-two minutes at the rate of six miles per hour. It would therefore have traveled approximately five miles or a little more. The river, being free from impediments, can be assumed to have brought the body down from a distance of five miles. Measuring back on the map it is apparent that the Gordon Ranch's *northwest* corner is just five miles from the dam. Had it come from the Wilson or Cosgrave ranches, the body would have arrived at the dam much later or sooner.

The murderer was never caught. The police, unfortunately, became confused and tried the Smith Ranch, which proved a dud. Later, on the Gordon Ranch they found the footprint record of a scuffle but were unable to fasten the crime on anyone in the vicinity. Molly was held guiltless.

No. 6
THE DUVENANT KIDNAPPING CASE

1. The kidnapper's car departed downhill, to the south. (Credit 3.)

2. Conclusive proof of the direction taken by the car is to be seen in the close-up drawing of the stud impressions in the tire track. It will be noted that in each stud the impression is sharper (that is, more deeply imprinted) at the end toward the bottom of the hill. It will be seen from the close-up of the tire track *on the level* that the impressions are of the same sharpness (that is, depth) at *both ends*.

Had the impressions of the studs been deeper at the end toward the top of the hill (the reverse of the way they were found), they would have indicated that the car had come uphill from the south and gone north. (Credit 7.)

This interesting subtlety in detective work is described by Melville Davisson Post in his excellent book, *The Man Hunters.* Mr. Post says:

> The Swiss police authorities assert that the direction taken by an automobile cannot be determined on a level road; but if one will follow an auto track until it begins to *descend a grade,* he can determine the direction the car has taken on the grade, provided the tires be studded. . . . As the car *descends* the hill the *anterior* part of the studs on the tire will be imprinted a little more deeply than the posterior part, or they will seem deeper by reason of the compression of the earth under the weight of the car on the studs as it advances.
>
> Thus, to discover the direction taken by a motor car one has only to follow the track to a grade and there ascertain whether it is the anterior or posterior part of the studs of the tire that are deeply imprinted on the dust, snow, or mud of the road.

By following the kidnapper's car downhill to the south, Detective Norcross and Duvenant were able to pick up the trail from various traffic policemen and attendants at gasoline filling stations. It led direct to the estate of Mrs. Duvenant's father in southern New Jersey. Jonathan was there!

To Duvenant's surprise, his wife's father insisted upon her returning the child at once, but Duvenant compromised, upon the father's signing a bond guaranteeing the safe keeping and return of the child, by letting her keep him for a week's visit. It is understood that the matter was settled out of court.

No. 7
THE LIGHTHOUSE TRAGEDY
AT DEAD MAN'S HARBOR

1. There could be only two explanations of the mystery at Dead Man's Harbor. Either the captain had deserted his post or he had met with foul play. M. Jacques believed the latter because he deduced that whoever had *left* the island by foot had taken pains to conceal his footprints, which he had done by dragging a board over them. The fact that this board had been dragged, obviously to efface footprints, since not a trace of a footprint remained, pointed to concealment and indicated a strong motive for mystifying the townspeople. The captain's boat was still on the island, so he couldn't have left in it. He had not been seen in the town, and there was no evidence that he had departed voluntarily. If the captain had suddenly become a victim of amnesia and had wandered off into the woods,

he would hardly have taken the precaution to conceal his footprints Everything considered it looked like foul play, especially since M. Jacques saw that a murderer could have done his deed, disposed of the body, and escaped, as will be seen later. (Credit 1.)

2. The murderer had probably reached the island in a boat on the incoming tide the night before – in all probability before eleven when the fog settled down. (Credit 2.)

3. The murderer disposed of the body of Captain Williams by putting it into the boat in which he had come to the island. He left the oars in the boat and set it adrift just as the tide began to go out again, knowing that the rush of the outgoing tide would carry the boat out to sea. A forty-foot tide necessarily moves *rapidly*, and the murderer took advantage of this. Undoubtedly he had planned to take the body off in his boat, but dared not risk getting lost in the fog. (Credit 2.)

4. The murderer escaped from the island by walking over the damp sand at low tide (dragging the board behind him to destroy footprints which otherwise would have indicated the direction taken). By doing so he completely mystified the local authorities. The murderer would undoubtedly have left the island much sooner, perhaps wading when only shallow water remained, except for the dense fog which hung

over the region. It is probable that he did not feel certain of finding his way in the fog to the ladder – the only means of ascent to the promontory at low tide. (Credit 3.)

5. The captain's body probably would be found in the boat, which might be picked up at sea by some vessel, or along the coast by fishermen. (Credit 2.)

Thirteen days after the disappearance of the captain a dead man in a small boat was picked up twenty-five miles out by a freighter *Water Nymph*. It was that of Captain Williams. He had been shot through the heart.

The small boat was brought to port. The name had been painted out, but careful removal of the obliterating coat of paint disclosed the name *Dodger*. This rather unusually named boat enabled the police to find and investigate its owner, a former seaman who had lived in the little town of Eatsport, Maine, for the previous ten months, doing odd jobs for the fish canneries there.

They found that the seaman, Jacobs, had sailed under Captain Williams on the captain's last voyage, more than twelve years before. The records showed that he had headed a mutiny which had been sternly put down by the captain. Several of the mutineers had been killed; Jacobs and two others had been brought home in irons and tried. Jacobs had received ten years in the Federal penitentiary. He confessed when cornered (having turned up in the police lineup at Scranton, Pennsylvania) that ever since his release he had been shadowing Captain Williams to "get him."

Jacobs was executed.

No. 8
WHO MURDERED ALGERNON ASHE?

1. Frederick Freeman, the American, husband of Mary Freeman, murdered Algernon Ashe at Monte Carlo. (Credit 1.)

2. The detective deduced it from the burned fragment of cardboard which he recognized as part of a dated weight card from a penny-in-the-slot machine. The Monte Carlo detectives had previously reasoned that this was probably drawn from the murderer's own pocket when he was in urgent need of something to ignite from his waning last match. Proceeding on this hypothesis, the famous detective deduced that the "228–230" on the fragment (meaning 228–230 pounds) fitted only Freeman. He alone of the men of the three suspected parties was tall and stout, according to the descriptions gleaned from the hotel attachés. It was more reasonable, therefore, to follow the Freemans to Paris than the others to Spain and Rome. (Credit 9.)

The printing on the back of the weight card also served to identify it. It appeared as possibly a part of the stereotyped "character reading" which slot machines in America commonly give for a penny in addition to one's weight. Stout persons, keeping close tabs on their variations in weight, are frequent patrons of such machines.

It came out subsequently that Freeman had suspected an affair between his wife and Ashe and had intercepted a letter to her sent that afternoon by the Englishman. The jealous husband had opened the envelope with a hot knife, had read the letter, and restored it to the envelope, and gummed down the flap again, so that his wife had no suspicion of the tampering. In the note Ashe had named a tryst for that evening in the gardens to discuss final plans for a proposed flight to India or Brazil. The tryst was for 9:30, a time of the evening when Freeman would customarily be at play at the casino tables.

Freeman said nothing. He went to the casino as usual but left early, and told his wife that urgent business demanded their presence in a Paris bank by the next day. He promised a quick return, however, and she, rather than arouse his suspicion, consented and began immediately to pack for the journey to Paris. Freeman then left to keep the appointment and shot down Ashe in cold blood. As he afterward admitted, Freeman searched the body hurriedly for letters from his wife, which he thought Ashe might be carrying in his pockets. He found three, which subsequently served to draw the net tighter when they were found in his possession.

Mrs. Freeman, when she wrote to Ashe explaining her inability to keep the appointment, feared to send the letter by messenger and mailed it instead. This the detectives got the next morning at Ashe's hotel.

Freeman was convicted but escaped with a nine-year sentence. Mrs. Freeman sued successfully for divorce and later married a French architect of Marseilles.

No. 9
Édouard Trimpi's Perplexing Dispatch

1. Trimpi had cleverly evaded the Spanish censorship and was therefore arrested, when it was discovered, by the Spanish authorities. (Credit 5.)

2. The gist of the *Chronicle's* scoop was: a revolution in Spain is imminent because of public discontent with the royalist government, and there has been a military outburst resulting in the capture of several hundred of the royalist soldiers who were trying to bolster up the government's position. It is unlikely that the fall of the royalist government can be averted because the populace is with the armed rebels. (Credit 5.)

Trimpi's position at the beginning of the outbreak in Barcelona was tantalizing. He happened to be there and happened to get the details of the important occurrence, but could send no news of it to his paper because of the strict government censorship. Therefore Trimpi took a chance on couching his dispatch in veiled language which might appear unimportant routine to the Spanish censors but would probably convey the news to his newspaper. By pretending that he was interviewing himself on technical financial details of stock market affairs he succeeded in doing this once, but was caught and arrested the second time.

Trimpi used "complete market overturn" for "revolution"; "accumulated lack of popular buying of *chair* shares" for "long growing discontent with the *throne*"; "sharp rise of steel" for "armed outbreak"; "operators" for "soldiers"; "curb buying with steel as favorite" for "popular support of the armed rebels."

When the editors of the *Chronicle* heard from the State Department of Trimpi's arrest, they comprehended the significance of his cable.

The revolution was unsuccessful, although for a time it seemed almost certain to succeed. Trimpi was released a week later upon request of the State Department, after promising not to attempt evasion of the Spanish censorship again.

No. 10
The Club Car Mystery at Syracuse

1. To locate Dennis Sloan, the brakeman of the train, a search should have been ordered for his dead or wounded or senseless body along the railroad line, probably *east* of Ford's Crossing. (Credit 3.)

2. Sloan's arrest as murderer of Capewell should *not* have been ordered. Sloan was undoubtedly a victim of the escaped murderer, as it is evident that the murderer *impersonated* the brakeman when Osborne tried to enter the car. (Credit 2.)

3. Sloan was not an accomplice. (Credit 1.)

4. The murderer, not Sloan, must have assaulted the porter. (Credit 2.)

5. In all probability, after the last call to dinner in the club car, at 7:30, Capewell and one other passenger (the murderer) remained in the car, as well as Johnson, the porter, and Sloan, the brakeman – the latter probably on the back platform, where a brakeman often stands. The murderer probably blackjacked the porter and brakeman, and then followed out his well-laid plan of murdering Capewell and throwing his body off the train.

The brakeman either fell off accidentally or was thrown off by the murderer, *after* the murderer had taken his coat and cap to wear in impersonating the

brakeman before Osborne, the passenger. The murderer undoubtedly escaped by jumping when the train
slowed down. He left the coat and cap, poorly concealed, to throw suspicion on the brakeman, though
this was probably an afterthought. (Credit 2.)

Captain McCumber has commented as follows on the
case:

> It's an unsolved mystery to-day because the
> detectives didn't recognize immediately that
> someone in the club car was impersonating the
> brakeman when Osborne tried to get in the club
> car. This should have been clear from two things:
> the "brakeman's" answer when Osborne asked
> him the time – "eight of eight." (No railroad
> man would have said that; he would have said,
> "7:52.") Also, the coat and cap in the drawer; if
> Sloan had wanted to hide them, he would have
> thrown them out of the train; obviously they
> were left there for a purpose: to throw some
> suspicion on the brakeman, or rather, to leave
> something which might be taken to explain
> what had happened.
>
> The real murderer of course jumped from
> the back platform when the train slowed down
> on approaching the yards of Syracuse. On the

outskirts of the city is where they should have looked for him. Instead of that, they leaped to the conclusion that Sloan had done it, and all the while poor Sloan was lying in the gully beside the embankment near Orrington with a broken leg and a bruised skull. Some track walkers found him two hours later.

I later questioned both Sloan and Johnson, the porter, soon after their recovery, but of course it was too late then: the murderer had had plenty of time to get away.

On the basis of what Sloan and Johnson told me, I reconstructed the happenings as follows:

The murderer had undoubtedly planned the crime, hoping to get Capewell alone on the back platform, shoot him, and throw him off at a time when the train was about to slow down. This would give him a chance to drop off with comparative safety and escape. Capewell, it seems, had had an early dinner and returned to the club car. Possibly he was dozing.

The murderer was probably unknown to Capewell, or was disguised. Soon after the other passengers went forward to the diner, he went to the front of the club car, where Johnson was looking out of the window, and struck the unsuspecting porter with a blackjack. All Johnson remembered was that something hit him from behind. Johnson could not tell me how many passengers had remained in the club car after the last dinner call.

Taking the porter's keys, the murderer locked the front door of the club car and drew down the curtain in its window. He then hurried, for he knew that passengers might be returning and seeking entrance to the car at any minute. Sloan, standing on the platform, was also struck from behind. He remembered only that. I imagine that the murderer then lured Capewell to the back platform, possibly by calling out that the brakeman had fainted and needed assistance; and when Capewell came to the platform and bent over the brakeman, shot him and threw his body off.

The murderer then heard the pounding and ringing of the impatient Osborne at the front door of the car. The train had not yet slowed down, but was due to slow down soon. From the murderer's point of view, therefore, it was imperative to stave off any investigation of the locking of the car, which might have resulted if the passenger had become disgusted and summoned a conductor.

Guessing that it was a passenger, but not

feeling sure, the murderer stripped the prostrate brakeman of his coat and hat, donned them and *peeked* out from behind the door-window curtain. When he saw that it was a passenger and not one of the train crew (who would have known him for an impostor), he unlocked the door and put Osborne off by saying the car was temporarily closed. To have refused an answer to Osborne's question: "What's the right time?" would have aroused more suspicion than to answer him. He did so, therefore, but not as a railroad man would certainly have said it. But this of course was lost on Osborne, and unfortunately on all of those who first investigated the case.

I am inclined to the belief that the murderer, upon re-locking the door and rushing to the back platform, found that the brakeman had fallen off from the swing of the train; but possibly he was more cold-blooded than I imagine and threw the unconscious brakeman off. At any rate, he saw the advantage of leaving the brakeman's coat and cap in the drawer, thereby implying that the brakeman had tried to conceal them. The train slowed down a few minutes later, and he undoubtedly jumped off and made his escape.

It was one of the coldest-blooded and most carefully planned murders I have ever investigated.

No. 11
THE MYSTERY OF HAJI LAL DEB

1. Mainwaring deduced Haji Lal Deb's probable guilt from his deception as to the time of the death of his aged relative. It seemed highly probable to Mainwaring that there must have been a *strong* motive for anyone to hold a plague-stricken body for two days before burying it. The coincidence of the holding of the body for burial and the disappearance of the rich merchant was highly suspicious. It indicated that Haji Lal Deb might have postponed burial of the body in order that the event might mask some other operation. And Mainwaring reasoned: Haji Lal Deb knew that holding the body was a suspicious act; therefore he lied and said that his relative had died *on the very night* of the disappearance of the merchant. (Credit 4.)

2. Mainwaring proved the guilt of Haji Lal Deb by digging up the ground directly *under* the body of the relative. There, four feet below the grave of the old man, lay the corpse of the merchant. (Credit 6.)

Haji Lal Deb had sought to fool the authorities and avert all suspicion by hiding the merchant's body in the one place where they would be the least likely to look for it after examining the topmost grave. He was immediately arrested and charged with the crime, and, although he protested his innocence, was convicted and executed.

Autopsy revealed that the merchant had been drugged with *dhatura*, an insidious Indian poison as easily made there as dandelion wine could be made in America. The *dhatura* flower is common in India, growing wild in the fields. A small dose of *dhatura* will stupefy the victim so effectively that he loses memory temporarily and can later tell nothing of what happened while under the influence of the drug. A large dose is fatal. It was substantially proved at the trial that Haji Lal Deb had drugged the merchant with *dhatura* mixed in a bowlful of rice, and had subsequently robbed him and stabbed him to death. Two hundred and forty rupees were later recovered from a cache under the roots of a wild plum tree in the vicinity of the hut of Haji Lal Deb.

In Mainwaring's opinion the death of the aged relative of his wife suggested to Haji Lal Deb a neat way of disposing of another body without much suspicion. He accordingly planned the murder of the merchant for robbery – a crime which, Mainwaring believed, he had long contemplated.

Charges against the wife as an accomplice broke down for lack of evidence.

No. 12
The Strange Case of the Promissory Note

1. The markings on the back of the yellowed document led Mrs. Mannington to suspect that something might be wrong because they were obviously *part* of some design which had been cut off of the sheet of paper. And if something had been cut off, it was reasonable to suspect that it might have been cut off for the purpose of concealment. (Credit 3.)

Mrs. Mannington noted especially that the only part of the mysterious markings remaining on the back of the piece of paper almost coincided with the position of the signature on the reverse side. These markings had to remain on the back if the signature on the reverse side was to remain. She suspected that otherwise they would have been cut off also.

2. In the opinion of all the lawyers and of Mrs. Mannington, Renoir had probably obtained the piece of paper from his deceased sister's autograph album which Mannington had at some time undoubtedly signed. (Credit 7.)

This they deduced cogently from the strange pen-and-ink markings on the back of the sheet on which

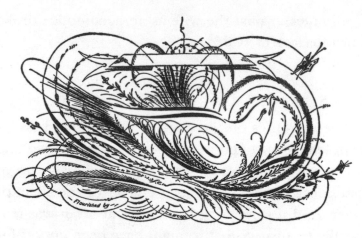

A typical "Flourish" – complete

An accomplishment of ladies and gentlemen during the Victorian era. Some of the designs were extremely elaborate and required considerable dexterity, for the work had to be done rapidly in order to achieve the desired dashing effect. The best "flourishers" were in great demand by every girl who possessed an autograph album, and most girls of that day had one.

the alleged promise to pay had been typed. In these finely stroked lines they recognized ends of pen strokes such as were used in making the elaborate "flourish" designs often inscribed in autograph albums in the latter part of the last century. In such albums some wrote verses; some "flourished" intricate designs of birds, flowers, etc.; some even painted little water colors; and those of lesser accomplishment merely signed their names, with date. Richard Mannington had been of this latter class. He had probably signed his name and the date in the center of a page in the album. The person next invited to inscribe in the album had "flourished" a design on the other side of the sheet, and it happened that the fringe of one side of the design nearly coincided with Mannington's signature on the reverse.

When Mr. Philip Renoir fell into possession of the album upon his sister's death, he probably saw in it an opportunity to forge a note over the signature of Mannington now grown wealthy. When Mannington died, the opportunity to prey on his widow became obvious to him. He clipped the page from the album and trimmed it down as much as he dared; then he typed in the "note."

Renoir was never caught. The San Francisco police department detective assigned to the case found that Renoir had consulted typewriting experts some months before as to the characteristic type on typewriting machines used in the early 'eighties. He had bought an ancient machine from one of the experts, saying that he desired it for his private museum of business appliances. With this Renoir undoubtedly forged the typed lines of the "note."

No. 13
The Death of Barnabas Frobisher

1. Barnabas Frobisher met his death at the hands of the butler, John Graves. (Credit 5.)

2. This is rather conclusively indicated by the powder marks on the backs of the victim's fingers (which preclude the theory of suicide) and by Graves's own denial of the possibility that an intruder could have slipped in and murdered Frobisher. Graves wanted it to look like suicide and set the stage accordingly, but did not notice the telltale powder marks on the backs of Frobisher's fingers. These of course indicated that Frobisher, threatened at close range, had clapped his hands over his eyes when he saw that escape was impossible. The powder had been blown into the skin of the backs of the fingers. Such marks would have been impossible if Frobisher had fired the revolver, and barring that, only Graves could have murdered Frobisher and set the stage. (Credit 5.)

A letter from Frobisher to his wife found in the slain man's strong box later revealed that he was being systematically blackmailed by Graves for considerable sums of money, and that he was mustering his courage to have his persecutor arrested. Graves, alias George Rhonda, a professional blackmailer, had secured proof of a serious violation of the Income Tax law by Frobisher some years before, and had taken a position as butler to be near his victim. He was so successful in intimidating his employer that more than $7,000 in cash had been paid by Frobisher. More had been demanded. Frobisher demurred. Graves had served an ultimatum for that evening. Frobisher sullenly put him off. Fearing that he had oppressed his victim so far that the worm was about to turn, Graves seized the opportunity offered by the cook's absence from the house and the passing of the fire engines, which would drown noise of the shot, and killed Frobisher without warning.

As he later confessed when captured at the railway depot, Graves removed his shoes in the pantry, stole up on his victim who was reading and shot him from the front. For this purpose he had taken Frobisher's own pistol from his bedroom upstairs. The butler then wiped his own fingerprints from the weapon, pressed it into the dead man's hand to register his fingerprints, and then laid it carelessly on the side of the seat of the chair. He then returned to the pantry, put on his shoes, walked in and out as if to discover the body, and then reported the crime to the police as a case of suicide.

Graves's insinuation to the police that Frobisher had committed suicide because of losses from speculation was cogent, since Frobisher, hiding his troubles from his wife, had been obliged to assign speculation as an explanation for his heavy spendings (for hush money). Graves played his whole game secure in the knowledge that there was a complete absence of apparent motive for the crime. Had it not been for the powder marks on the backs of his victim's fingers, he might have escaped the constant shadowing which resulted later in his arrest as he was preparing to leave the city.

Graves was convicted the following April and was hanged.

No. 14
The Problem of the Amnesia Case

1. The amnesia victim had once worked in San Francisco at the time of the earthquake of 1906. This is commonly referred to as "the San Francisco fire," since most of the damage resulted from fire. (Credit 7.)

2. He had probably been a press telegrapher. His mention of "trunks" referred to trunk *wires*, not packing trunks. "Thirty" is the telegraph operator's signal for the end of a dispatch. It has come to have a general connotation of finality among telegraph and newspaper men. (Credit 3)

Perhaps the most definite indication of where the amnesia victim had worked was found in his phrase:

"They always made you say it was fire." The irony of the enforced euphemism in describing the San Francisco disaster of 1906 had evidently made a deep impression on the mind of the amnesia victim at that time.

No. 15
THE HUPPENHEIMER MUSEUM ROBBERY

1. Two men were guilty in the Huppenheimer Museum robbery. There is no evidence that more than two were guilty. (Credit 2.)

2. Assistant Curator Raymond was the directing genius of the robbery; Antonio Diaz, whose coat was captured, was his confederate who did the actual taking of the real gems. (Credit 3.)

3. The robbery was carried out in the following manner:

On the day of the Prince of Wales's visit the Assistant Curator deceived Curator Waltham. He did not remove the real jewels to the safe, but *left them in the case*. He put the paste replicas in the safe and falsely reported to the curator that orders had been carried out as given.

Diaz, the confederate, made his appearance the following day and began copying the design of the Rurik jewels in order to make a dummy set. Diaz was also studying the case and the "lay of the land" on the second floor of the museum.

Answer Section

Diaz was not yet ready for the robbery when the Assistant Curator was suddenly ordered to New York by Curator Waltham on an emergency errand. This fit in splendidly with the Assistant Curator's desire to avoid any tangible suspicion of complicity: the robbery should be done in his *unexpected* and *involuntary* absence, and then he believed that he would scarcely be suspected of having a hand in it. But he must let Diaz know.

Therefore, as soon as the Assistant Curator received orders to go to New York immediately, to be gone from Friday until Tuesday, he dispatched instructions to his confederate in their prearranged code, to hurry and take advantage of the situation. (Credit 2.)

4. Guilt was proved by Raymond's code message, ingeniously contrived to appear as an innocent column of figures. It was probably tapped off on an adding machine available in the museum executive offices. The code was a numerical one, and the message read:

ORDERED N.Y. TILL TUESDAY STRIKE SOON.

The letters of the alphabet were numbered 1 to 26, starting at Z, and printed two letters to a line with a decimal point between, except where two numbers lower than 10 came together and would make a number larger than 26, when they were written as one number: for instance, 7 (T) and 6 (U) were written as 76. Detective Wagner deciphered the message as follows:

```
12-9-23-22-9-22-23   13-2   7-18-15-15
 O  R  D  E  R  E  D   N Y   T  I  L  L

7-6-22-8-23-26-2   8-7-9-18-16-22   8-12-12-13
 T  U  E  S  D  A Y   S  T  R I  K  E   S  O  O  N
```

(Credit 3.)

Assistant Curator Raymond hanged himself in his cell the day following his arrest, and "Antonio Diaz" was never found. His identity, however, was learned, and this threw some light on the strange affair. "Diaz" was none other than Porfirio Butler, scapegrace son of Dr. Simeon Butler, the English Argentinian gem expert and one-time Director of the Buenos Aires Public Museum. Together the foreigner and Raymond had probably planned the sale of the celebrated pieces under some ingenious guise – possibly to some South American museum or to a wealthy private collector.

It was the essence of Raymond's scheme to have the robbery appear to have been done by an outsider. Trading on his reputation, which up to that time had been good, the Assistant Curator would say that he had not mixed the real and false gems – and what could be done about it? At the worst his superiors could accuse him of carelessness. This he would deny vigorously and leave in any detective's mind the implication that any one of the three men who had the combination of the safe might have been an accomplice. But his confederate's carelessness in keeping the coded note in his coat pocket proved their downfall.

Curator Waltham resigned, a broken man. Dr. Oddie, however, exonerated him of all blame. It later developed that Raymond had been something of a Dr. Jekyll and Mr. Hyde. Several persons who had been the victims of forgeries at Raymond's hands during his youth came forward when the scandal came out.

The Rurik pieces were never entirely recovered. Three of the smaller amethyst rings were found in a London pawnshop some years later; and two of the large gold bracelets turned up in a private collection in St. Louis.

They are now kept in the museum safe *all* the time.

THE END